CAVERN

CITY IN THE DARK

by

NICHOLAS MORINE

Cavern: City in the Dark

by Nicholas Morine.

Featuring an illustration by Jesse H. Walker.

ISBN-13: 978-1-927996-01-0

Published by Problematic Press.

To purchase copies of this book, please visit: http://problematicpress.wordpress.com

Printed in the United States.

Cover image: Francisco Goya's *War Scene* (1812).

The hat logo is a trademark of Problematic Press.

Table of Contents

There are some who are in darkness

And the others are in light

And you see the ones in brightness

Those in darkness drop from sight

— "Mack the Knife," Bertolt Brecht

BOOK 1:

THE PRESENT

CHAPTER 1: THE WATCHER

The Sufferer sat beneath the tree of tears. Old, wizened skin, dark and gnarled like a tree root, his bare hands and feet showing from beneath a rough patchwork robe. Stone still, statuesque, apparently immortal. Appearances were often deceiving. His costume was his simple robe and withered skin, face obscured. Beyond him and the tree, a glowing city, enshrouded in light and darkness of every shade and hue. The Sufferer and the tree of tears shared a cage built from steel and glass.

For when his heart breaks, pain would once again be felt by all. The conduit would collapse and each man and woman would once again be an island.

So was the way of things. The Elite whom governed the city had seen it before. Had smothered it twice in living memory.

The Watcher knew that by even thinking such things, his fear and anxiety would be shunted off into The Sufferer, perhaps even hastening his death — yet he could not summon the passion to care. Nor even the inclination, now that he thought about it. His role as representative for the cavern city, the last living outpost, demanded his perfect attention to detail. And duty. He could feel his shunt working away the worry, nibbling at his perfect attention. His costume was a space-black laboratory coat emblazoned with proud symbols and a loose ponytail. He was observing the Sufferer, taking in the scars and the deep lines of age that folded his skin. The icon of serenity, the Watcher thought to himself, tapping his foot against the floor outside of the cage impatiently.

Life was perfect amongst the Flawless; The Watcher had been their ambassador to the Old One for his entire life amongst his other duties. Surveillance, crowd control, rehabilitation, termination — in other words, security, along with his partner The Huntress. For decades they'd ensured the continuation of the greatest culture history had ever known. With Huntress at his side, they'd been the stewards of over a century of peace.

Pax perfectus. Perfect peace. For generations.

Flawless. The foundational truth of life in the cavern for generations. Hanging on each rust-lunged, rattling breath breaking past the lips of the old man under the tree.

Thoughts of failure were shunted away from his cerebral cortex by the physical hardware at the base of his brain. The shunt. That's what everyone called it who was not a scientist; the multi-syllabic model name didn't quite roll off the tongue. He was aware of his cyberbiology, detached, beyond fear – sending all primitive negativity downstream even as his intellect could conjure these thoughts. He forcibly shut down this line of thinking, digging fingernails into soft palms and squinting his bespectacled eyes shut.

"Problems, Professor?"

Professor Okona Okozaki – The Watcher – was caught off guard, flinching awkwardly.

"Did I startle you?"

The voice was hard and low with only slight whispers of femininity. The Huntress stepped past the indignant professor, gliding long tapered fingers thoughtfully along her jawline. Bemusement twinkled beneath grey-black eyes.

"The fact that you escape my powers of detection today does not mean that you will tomorrow, Marli."

Weakness was anathema in the cavern city, threats becoming common masks.

"I will again tomorrow, my friend," The Huntress said. "How is The Sufferer faring?" She stepped forward to lean against the glass ring outlining the old one's chamber, gaze narrowing in scrutiny.

"He is beyond any medical intervention. In fact, there's really nothing wrong with him. No signs of poison, or genetic manipulation away from his genotype. No disease or sickness. His replacement heart is fully operable, as are the arterial reinforcements the nanos implanted."

"Yet he's going to die?" she asked.

"The scientists at the university as well as our own think tank bio-engineers say he's got about a month. Give or take a week or so. That's barely enough time to prepare a replacement."

A beat.

"I will begin an immediate screening process of my

current holdings, and prepare a roster of superior candidates for your selection, Professor," she said.

The Watcher shifted his weight and scratched at the back of his head, thinking. His slick black leather lab-coat was formfitting against his lean, skeletal frame. It was embroidered with the logo of Cavern City – an angular linkage suggesting mechanical solidarity – above the LED script bearing his name and official title.

The Huntress studied him coolly, her own garments a snow white contrasting against his. Her costume was criss-crossed with bright crimson embroidery in a personal damask, fitted and armoured. When the rare Flawed suspect put up a fight, Huntress was eager to put them down. It felt good; she enjoyed it. Her lovers often reaped the rewards, though the Professor was rarely interested in such carnal delights and distractions. A pity, she thought.

When he failed to reply, remaining transfixed in his observation of the dying vessel, Marli coughed and scuffed a booted foot impatient to break the professor's reverie.

"Yes, yes. Flawed candidates make the best sufferers; they last about twice as long. It's been years since we've used one of our own, hasn't it?" he said, scouring his memories and coming up with a murky blank.

"This one has lasted the longest by far," she said.

"Yes, truly formidable. Nothing notably superior about him genetically. Does cause one to wonder..." he trailed off.

"Wonder? I think it's just pure luck. The Flawed are so afraid to die that they'll do anything to avoid it. Could be that the old man here is just too afraid to see what's on the other side. We picked a perfect coward is my theory," she said dismissively.

Theoretical strings never really did much to excite her, much to the Professor's chagrin; she made relatively poor conversational company despite her obvious assets to their government. The Huntress, The Mouth, himself, and a half dozen others in lesser administration and liaison positions. Flawless, and representatives of their society, the best on offer. Politicians were popular under Flawless rule; positive improvements were recognized and progress was never halted by disagreement or debate.

All was well and incumbency had many rewards.

"I don't think so. There's something strange about this one."

"Superstition from a scientist? Things really are starting to get a little heavy, aren't they?" she raised an eyebrow and turned, leaning against the glass.

He snorted in reply. "It's not superstition – you said it yourself. This one has endured a great deal longer than any others."

"Like I said, fear is a great motivator. We wouldn't know."

He nodded, scrutinizing his console.

"You know, I'm having dreams," he said.

A perceptible pause.

"Dreams?" she asked.

"Dreams. You know. Visions while I sleep."

"Right..." Huntress moved her hands down casually to the hilts of her twin kukri, twin machetes burnished to a near chrome finish.

"Rarely," he reiterated. "I chalked them up to overwork

but I now address them as empirical evidence."

Her grip loosened, though her fingers stilled touched the pommel. "Evidence. Nothing personal, then? You're not feedback sick?"

The Watcher turned at the waist, smiling wryly at her. A lock of his hair fell loose and swung like a pendulum in front of his nose.

"Really, Marli. You've known me for how long? Quit it with the big shot play."

Her hands fell loose, resting akimbo.

"Better safe than sorry. You've got nothing to worry about if you've got nothing to hide. The constitution, remember?" she said, crossing her arms.

"I hide nothing. See what I disclose to you? I do not do this lightly." … grinding his teeth.

Countered by a lilting, spritely laugh.

"I know it, Okona. There are many stories circulating. The people speak of these… dreams. These… visions." Huntress was pacing, stopped, and turned her head to the side.

"I have not experienced them myself... but too many report the symptoms for it to be pure coincidence. It must be the imminent death of The Sufferer," she said.

"When he dies we will already have a replacement." A keening whine split his skull. He raised his right hand to his temple and staggered, bracing himself against the edge of the console.

The Huntress stalked from the chamber, her steel-toed boots clanging against the burnished grating of the laboratory, the pinnacle sanctum. Her white cape trailed behind her.

CHAPTER 2: SILVERTONGUE AND SONG

The stream studio was simple, clean, corporate. A simple 20x20 soundstage, a few lights cast from above, and warmer peripheral pots to soften the edges. A wall monitor behind the cherrywood news desk — some status symbols clung to life despite generations of postmodernity. A small crew of aides manning the dual mobile cams, acquiring 3D and in-camera correcting by the millisecond.

The Mouth sat confidently behind the ochre majesty of the antique anchor's desk. His handsome, sun-warmed features were split in a gracious grin as he spoke offstage to the senior set aide. His salt and pepper hair was combed into a perfect coif. The lighting was a bit too harsh, adding years to his middle-aged face. It dimmed appropriately. His costume was a reflective silver suit, complimented by the finest silk shirt in a baby blue, a white tie overtop.

"Lights are better, sir. Optimal aesthetics have been acquired. Ready to stream whenever you are," the set boss called out in a hushed tone.

"Good, good. Got any news on the big story?"

"Just what was in your briefing notes from The Professor, sir."

The Mouth nodded slightly and then returned to his own pose, gesturing towards the far corner of the set for a glass of water. A small and wiry young man in an ill-fitting sportcoat scrambled forward with a pitcher and glass in hand, retreating just as quickly as he had come. The anchorman brushed his wavy, greying hair back with his hand, using the other to tilt his desk tablet to make it easier to consult without being too obvious.

"Ten seconds, and..." the main grip said, and the silent countdown began. A warm and self-confident smile spread over The Mouth's countenance, liquid honey poured over a plastic mould. His eyebrows at the perfect arch between expressing wonder and joviality. Wrinkles wiped away and blended under makeup and post-processing. He knew it all; his book on the subject was the national standard.

A brief hand signal from the rear assistant told him it was gametime. The wall monitor sprang to life without delay, an immense projection of a new residential / financial development filling the entire field of view behind the news desk. Camera 1 elongated, swinging on its arm around the wallscreen, panning and zooming over this borough and that in dramatic fashion. It helped to disorient the view slightly and to better bring them into the program. *Half of successful streaming was psychology*, after all. The leading sentence in his book and an excellent soundbyte for the talk and business sermon circuit.

"Good evening citizens of Cavern — what a wonderful evening out there tonight — my name is Alan Scarlet. This program is brought to you by The Megapass — *streaming your life daily*." He tilted his head cameraside to show greeting and continued.

"Flawed persons continue to hassle enforcement officers and citizens passing by in increasing numbers, internal statistics show. In Brookside, incidents of harassment from Flawed individuals have risen 20% in Davislet and a full 39% in the Periphery." His unblemished brow furrowed. His eyes took on a steely glint. The Periphery, the erratic and tumbledown neighbourhoods that clung to the edge of Cavern, was a constant source of trouble for the Elite.

17

The Mouth took a brief breath, then continued in his stentorian singsong.

"Authorities assure all that the installation of a new catalyst will take place within the next 48 hours, reducing truancy and relapse rates to their previous floor at a subpercentile level. Of course, in the interim, it is required of all Flawless citizens to report truancy wherever suspected; you'll see the PIN and email at the bottom of your stream. It has been saved to your personal clouds for your convenience."

Three dimensional film was piped into the stream. An enormous arena was displayed, countless people cheering in the stands, the seats themselves staggering up until they resembled nothing but a coloured, tapering ribbon into the exposed night sky. The roar was deafening, or would be without dampers, loud and saturated. Dressed in a wild style, the crowd was a carnivale couture. Ruffled lace juxtaposed with fiber-optic infused leathers. Silk scarves edged in razorblades and bone. Full LED suits slinging personal advertisements for sushi, pizza, beer, and pharma. Homespun yarns bedecked in beads and business cards. The orgiastic nudes, writhing in clumps, insensitive, inattentive exhibitionists. All were paying customers.

On the fields below, a hundred battles raged. Men and women struggled in mortal combat against one another, bolstered by the catcalls of their audience and ambitious promise. Two women near the eastern edge of the stadium ducked and skulked behind rocks and root formations in a small ravine, firing pistols at one another. One was bleeding profusely from a ragged wound on her hip. Blood brought attention in the form of bets, donations, and new fans. Spoils for the victor as well as for the defeated, if she was valorous enough.

The main attraction was a raised dais in the absolute center of the arena. An object resembling a twentieth century wrestling or boxing ring, with two warriors circling each other, one trailing a hand along the ropes and turnbuckle as she eyed her prey.

The Huntress stood tall and proud, her muscular and angular body representing challenge to her opponent; a large and swarthy man with the physique of a professional bodybuilder. It seemed an uneven match if one was unfamiliar of the history of the martial forms. The Huntress very rarely competed in such crude competition — she was an Elite, after all — but as yet was undefeated in her appearances. Her opponent could say the same. He was The Champion and had been for a number of months. His costume was minimal, a simple pair of yellow wrestling trunks and boots, to accentuate the rigid, rock hard musculature of his six-foot-six frame. She wore the same white cotton and crimson that was her hallmark, the armor plating removed from sewn pockets.

Yet the odds lay in her favour, even amongst the loosest betting corps.

"The Huntress herself deigned to compete in this evening's celebrations, causing quite a stir by challenging the Champion himself to an exhibition match. Of course, not being on the official martial roster, The Huntress is not eligible to hold the title," The Mouth said, his voice disembodied over the streamed experience.

Artificial intelligence apps, realtime camera analysis software, projected the Huntress' power level at approximately 14.2 standards, or average persons. The champion's rating over the past season had been closer to eleven with spikes up to 12.4, a historic high topped only by The Mountain's record of 12.8. Of course, The Huntress was an elite — her edge even amongst the Flawless was perceptible.

An edited version reviewing the highlights of the struggle was shown. It had been relatively short and lopsided.

The Champion eventually rushed forward first to engage, catching The Huntress by surprise as he struck a glancing blow with his fist across her cheek. He paid for his recklessness by taking a counter-kick to the short ribs as he passed by. This time, Huntress moved forward with a flurry of punches and elbows, overwhelming the slower grappler's defense. A few jabs broke through and caught the hulking man on the jaw and neck, staggering him back.

A dissolve cut minutes from the interim. Now, the Champion was behind The Huntress, having placed her in a weak choke that she was working to break. He was cut and bruised, deep rivulets of sweat and blood poured from his face and upper body. His legs trembled and shook with exertion in tandem with the rise and fall of his great chest. The Huntress looked mussed and somewhat tired, a few cuts marked her arms and a few light bruises spotted her forearms, but she looked little worse for the wear.

Suddenly, she broke free of his hold by driving both of her elbows down into the tender muscles atop his thighs, already shaking with weakness. He bellowed a great cry of pain and released her, falling awkwardly forward onto his knees. Spinning artfully behind him by pivoting, The Huntress delivered a hammerfist to the side of The Champion's head, knocking him immediately unconscious. He slumped over as dead weight onto the stained canvas of the ring mat as the cheers of the crowd rained down onto The Huntress, her pure white outfit stained with blood to match. The audio of the cheers were dimmed over the celebrating victor.

"There is no shame to losing to The Huntress in such a worthy contest," The Mouth smoothly announced. "The Champion was seen to immediately and is expected to make a full recovery within the week, returning to action in two. The event drew record attendance," and here, the stream displayed a birds-eye 3D, "the megapass was pushed to 96% load and the old transit swiftubes were used by those who wished to dodge the historic traffic. All proceeds from the event will be applied to relapse rehabilitation efforts."

The arena faded away softly and the stream returned to the soft focus of The Mouth's soundstage. Again, he displayed a winning smile and bright white teeth.

"Moving to law enforcement news, a major relapse cell was recovered today in a suspect area of the cavern." The second motion camera swung on its rail behind him to focus on the wallscreen, which changed to project a map of The Silver Side district. "Silver Side borough is adjacent to the fashion and academic districts, an unlikely choice to say the least. I remind our viewers that relapse to a Flawed state is not a crime, it is a medical problem which requires rehabilitation – rectification. Please do not panic."

His smile widened.

"The relapse cell in question was comprised of nearly a hundred members; the sting took nearly a year to co-ordinate in order to ensure that all Flawed were accounted for when medical standards teams were dispatched."

It was a rare treat for streamers to see recent feeds from the Periphery; they were a notoriously secretive seat of black market power, particularly when it came to technology, and only rarely allowed media drones to so much as fly through their shadowy space. The Spire area, the entertainment districts, Cavern City proper presented a strong and stable seat of order, and no citizen could doubt that happiness and freedom from worry was now the norm, no matter which district they called home. So long as their shunts were functional and they stayed free of the underground, the alleyways, and the Periphery they would remain safe forever.

"Beautiful, isn't it?" The Mouth allowed himself to extol dreamily, disembodied, almost as if sitting comfortably next to the viewer. "Just look at the craftsmanship. The ability to blend the natural and the artificial without diminishing either." The Mouth was right; it was breathtaking. Long, toothlike stalactites and stalagmites jutted forth from the ceilings and floors of the subterranean chamber. Built onto their sides, in irregular and organic colonies were the structures of Cavern, each bearing a soft glowing light of their own choosing. Together, their lights created a permanent soft glow. The rock structures themselves were bioluminescent, quartz veins injected with a chemical compound that granted them an indefinite lifespan by mysterious means. The hustle and bustle of business was absent — most of the city was under a deep slumber.

Slowly, the camera found its point in the Periphery, a sliver of silver light wedged at the fringe of busier and more colourful districts, and approached.

Kettled into a small box, pressed up against stone walls by white and red robed enforcement officers, a group of men and women were screaming and shouting. Although their words were indeterminable their faces spoke volumes. Hatred, anxiety, and notably fear. Emotions foreign to the Flawless and foundational to the Flawed.

The camera whirred in closer on soundless wings. Close ups of their faces, contorted in agony as they were pressed against the cold brickwork, their arms wrenched behind their backs. The benign, smiling faces of the enforcers as they lashed the wrists of the wayward ones. Tears running down the face of an eight year old girl, clinging to the leg of a woman who appeared to be her mother, looking down at her with an urgent, plaintive expression. The sounds of cursing and sobbing, pulled down to a murmur by the aide manning the studio monitor. He flicked his gaze up to meet The Mouth's eyes, giving him the nod to proceed.

"87 relapsed individuals were rounded up in this early morning intervention yesterday; streaming is enabled now that the individuals have safely entered their rehab facility. It's important for streamers to remember that all relapsed individuals are treated fairly and humanely in every and all instances, and with a *greater than 99%* reintegration rate, most of us know at least one brother or sister who has been Flawed before. They're happier now; ask them yourselves!"

With his tonal flourish and finale, the camera whirled away from the silverlit crime-scene and flitted through tight, labryrinthine, organic corridors of the city's alleyways. Clotheslines stretched between tall and tilting buildings at irregular angles. Children's drones, toy remotes, and mailcarriers likewise floated through the air, dodging the weblike clotheslines with preprogrammed ease. The odd corpse of an unlucky or poorly piloted craft was strung up and silhouetted against the lights from nearby patios or unshuttered windows.

Classical strings and percussion, light and brassy, began to rise from the near silence of the stream through the cave city, lending the journey a spiritual sense. This chorus melted into a customized synthetic symphony, an epic from the preferred genre of each individual streamer's profiled psychology, stirring something within each of them.

The camera came over a low rooftop and a populated amphitheatre came into view, carved into the floor of the cavern. Curved rows of seating wound around and upward in risers, like the surface mines from the times of the ancients. A stage cut square was backed against the flat and phosphorous glow of the cave wall. Intricate stonework was overlayed like lattice, a beautiful backdrop for this evening's performance. The crowd was filled with the gurgle of mass chatter; many turned to point at the bright lights of the camera as the unit swung overhead.

Almost as if from thin air, a tall and slender woman appeared on the stage, wearing a pure white dress. Fitted and exquisitely tailored, it was modest yet elegant, displaying the toned muscles of her arms and legs without advertising anything further. Her face was angular, chiseled, refined, and intelligent – lips painted a dusky rose. Darkness reached for her, the natural cloak of the subterranean, and yet the persistent lights painted her as a human canvas, spectral, surreal. Blues, oranges, reds, purples, and vibrant greens touched her, flickering over her, staying a moment here and there. The camera focused upon her and the cheers of the crowd died to murmurs and then were extinguished into easy silence.

The Mouth appeared next to her, fading in from nothingness, wearing a new suit made from glossy black material, like cut coal or onyx. His costume was immaterial. A stage microphone burst into life in his hands, the top catching the morphing expressions of the colourful lights like a faceted diamond. The crowd was spellbound.

"Ladies and gentlemen of Cavern, and those watching the stream from around the city."

A dramatic pause.

"We welcome you. We welcome you to a night that will surely be remembered for all time. This memorable occasion that we celebrate tonight is the life and death of The Sufferer. A celebration, if you will, of all that we have accomplished with the catalyst installed — from pitiful beginnings in the muck and the dirt to the glory that we call Cavern today."

Pride was bursting in their throats and they hammered it forth in throaty cries, a literal wave of sound washed over the stage and through the ghosts upon it. Not just in the amphitheatre but rippling, resoundingly, throughout the entire cave and the city beyond. Apartments, alleyways, and gated communities rang out with the voices of the Flawless as they came together in emotional effervescence. Emotions ran higher than ever, matching spirits in flight, driving suffering underfoot.

"We have had our great games! We have seen our victors! The victorious Huntress! The noble Champion, survives! We have overcome so much together. The Sufferer represents all that is positive about the progress we have made; without the catalyst, we would return to the darkest days, the days of our ancestors, out there on the surface. A life replete with pain and chaos and disorganization, foreign to us, artifacts now of intellectual debate rather than present realities. This is a day of remembrance of the necessity and of the absolute beauty of the gift that our catalyst has given to us."

To the thunderous claps and bellows, "Thank you. And enjoy. The elite present to you, the most talented and beautiful songstress in living memory – Sirenia!" The Mouth left the stage with a sweeping hand, exiting the frame. His ghost was gone, a memory, leaving only the white-clad woman, holding nothing.

She began to sing.

She sang, her voice high and strong and proud, of things that most of them had never felt. Sadness, despair, worthlessness, sickness of the mind. Beatific and beautiful, the words poured forth like water on glass, the audience rising along with her to observe this symphony of suffering. A piano accompanied her syllables in perfect tune and timing. Hypnotized, the live audience and those experiencing the stream sat enraptured.

It was a tale of woe, woven partly from truth and partly from memory. The burning times. The times of pure darkness, the death of their arts. Savagery leading to more savagery until finally very few remained, isolated. The rebuilding times. The return of technology. The return of the lights to their dens. The advent of the shunt implant, the stream that allowed them to share so much. The device which gave them the ability to select their catalyst. The Sufferer. A vessel to contain every last bit of darkness that might stain their souls, contaminate their culture, give rise to rebellion and unrest and bloodshed.

She sang then of the primitive times, her voice becoming harsher and broken. Times when millions died and billions slaved for scraps while a meager few enjoyed a life worth living. She sang of a time when husbands and wives lived in guilt and shame over sins rather than to have perfect company and companionship. She sang of a world of lost opportunities and lies.

This was their world without their savior. As one vessel dies, one vessel must take their place. She sang this final truism, and it resonated within all of them as it shook the spiky formations accenting above and below, amplified.

Her voice quivered, wavered, and died.

There were long seconds of nothing but silence, the vacuum of the underground. Then, a maddening roar. Explosive pinwheels shooting sparks and smoke and lances of laser light cutting through the darkness. A crushing howl of exultation from the crowd as everyone was overwhelmed with joy and perfect acceptance of the suffering of their chosen catalyst, a vessel that had given so many years of service. A future restored after tumultuous times that had driven a wedge – though none would admit it – between them. Those in the stream executive offices opened the wine and set to celebrating.

The first Selection in a very long time. Revitalization and renewal for all. Years added to their lives and those years would be filled with nothing but the best that life had to offer. Each of them a personal hero or heroine, charged with purpose and invigorated, inspired. Progress would be swift; in no time they would conquer their problem of the cave and return *up there*. Sweep the dust from the scarred surface and reclaim what had been lost by staring too long into the abyss.

CHAPTER 3: SCALPELS

The camera panned away from the singer with soft strings, returning to focus on The Mouth in his studio as analysis of this evening's event took place. Panelists wearing perfectly pressed suits materialized in chairs aside his own cherrywood desk and began blabbering.

Those watching on the flatscreen turned away, some huffing in disgust.

They were inside a shipping container. The doors were unhinged and swung slightly shut, letting a crack of moist cave air inside. Stacks of containers sat one upon the other at the foot of the megapass, shoved in at random. Place had been named after the sprawl, the trainyard. Even here in the shadow of a shadow, most were content – but not all. As the hours ticked away and the shuntstream grew weaker with the failing of the catalyst, a palpable anxiety settled over the broken and rusting steel homes like fog. Most people were focused on the celebrations, the installation of the new catalyst; the weakening of the shunts only served to heighten their manic excitement.

Their group was four. A woman, tall and powerfully built, athletic. Straight black hair pulled into a ponytail over glinting green eyes. Shadows almost obscuring her ruby red leather duster, beaten and scuffed. A pair of leather leggings fit into dark motorcycle boots. Her old Yamaha Frankenstein was chained up outside. Her costume was not a costume. Her expression was one of disgust, her attractive face contorted, lips curled.

Her partners shared a variety of expressions nearby.

A short, round, scientific looking type wearing a similar black tech-slick as the elites – Turncoat. He'd brought her the information she'd needed, the thread that began to unravel. She only trusted him because there was no other option.

Pounding a small fist into palm and grinding it idly, teeth clenched and eyes alight with anger, the youngest member of their gang showed uncharacteristic anger. A teenage girl at the precipice of puberty, gangly and lean but not yet a woman, even if she was one in mind. Cropped-close hair and a mixed-race appearance lent her an exotic look, Lill was a student by trade. Little Mountain, her full name, was on the honour roll despite her interest in the occult, the forbidden. Her discoveries had driven her into the arms of their conspiracy.

The last, but not the least, was her father: The Mountain. Tall at six feet, but particularly broad at two hundred and sixty pounds, his Asiatic features showed little to no emotion as he sat, eyes closed, listening to the broadcast without watching. He had only recently been removed from the mainstream and was still attempting recovery after his rescue. His frame was hidden beneath the expanse of a cheap black suit, a body that used to be well muscled but had been neglected. A long curved blade rested against debris in the corner next to his chair.

"It was stupid of them to show their faces. The faces of our brothers and sisters," Lill spat out, barely able to contain herself, wiping away tears. She had a classmate disable her shunt after her discovery in the university library. Buried deep within the stacks was a black leatherbound tomb bearing arcane symbols. Not entirely unusual given her predilection for provocative study on subjects of unease. That book had changed everything for them. Made it all *make sense.*

"Yeah, you're right!" Turncoat said, nervously. "I can't believe they don't realize what they're doing... if people who have become flawed saw that footage, there's no going back for them. They're with us now. Right?"

"Nothing is certain," Domina said, wrangling the anger that ripped at her insides. The curl of her lip subsided as she began to plot a course of action. Time was certainly something in short supply; it appeared that the establishment was moving quickly to find a suitable replacement for The Sufferer. When that happened, everything they had worked for – and that many had died for – would be lost.

"Except for one thing," Lill pointed out, raising a small finger. "We cannot allow them to proceed with Selection."

This time it was Turncoat's turn to snort, unable to contain his disbelief. "You seriously think we're going to be able to stop the Elite? Take a look around; there's four of us. You're a kid – no offense, a smart kid – and I'm not much good in a fight." The rest was unspoken, leaving the aging and tired Mountain and their leader, Domina to dwell on it.

The Domina of Pain. The Red Lady. "Her." The one you need to find when you wake up. Screaming, crying, fearful – when you woke up, you looked for "her." Most never made it, ferreted out by innumerable and immaculately placed plants posing as confidants. Your friends and family members, false. Employees of a flawless system. And if you never woke up, you never needed to know.

Was it better to wake?

Domina was the only one who had never asked herself that question in the quiet of the night, the early morning hours when silence dominates. The stream, the flatscreen, the fan – white noise can only drown out so many thoughts that wander through the unshunted mind. With nowhere to go downriver, the natural poisons of the intellect begin to take hold again.

She knew nothing else. They had all known something else. She had been born illegally, had never known the steel touch of the shunt inside of her skull. That was how you would know it was her. She could show you the bare and unbroken spot at the base of the brainstem. No surgeon no matter how skilled could prevent the evidence of such an invasive surgery from view.

She was blind to the stream, understood it only as a figment apart, a communicative reality rather than a personal connection or a unity. She saw it on the flatscreen, heard it through the speakers. The others saw this eccentricity as inspiring, their own addictions to the comfort of the stream a shameful nonsecret. After a life of acclimation, day in and day out, of the sensory datastream it was difficult if not impossible to immerse oneself voluntarily after losing the shunt. Even if it was through the pale imitation of a projection, a wallscreen.

"Obviously, if Selection is completed, we lose all hope of ever returning life to our brothers and sisters. And we'll all be dead," she said.

"... Even if we were captured? What about rehab?" Turncoat's voice shook.

At this, Mountain startled them all, laughing harshly. "For a scientist, sir, you lack wisdom. Too much faith in what is seen, I think." This is all he would say, although now a smile graced his lips as he leaned back in the chair, eyes shut.

"There's no going to rehab for any of us, Turncoat," Domina said simply.

The flatscreen speakers continued to call out as The Mouth made his denouement.

Oh, what a time of celebration! Planned parties will be listed throughout the evening, with a week of holiday declared for all citizens immediately!...

At this you could nearly hear the entire city shiver with jubilation and the first hints of intoxication.

... and a full year of exemption from excavation and clearing duty as expansion gets put on hiatus. It's time to enjoy ourselves, don't you think folks? As always, it has been truly wonderful to spend this time with you. If you'd like to see more of me, be sure to sign up for our streaming archive service. Free of charge from me to you. See you at the party, folks.

"Tonight it is, then."

Even The Mountain raised an eyebrow, though he didn't bother to open his eyes. Turncoat sputtered while Lill laughed uncomfortably.

"Tonight?" Lill asked. "You can't be serious. We aren't ready. It's just us and the four other cells. We haven't even begun to plan this, Domina."

"I'm afraid..." Turncoat began.

"Of course you are," Domina sneered, cutting in.

"...I'm afraid that I have to agree with our youngest member here. This is suicide. You might be the leader but—"

"But what, boy?" Domina rasped, taking a booted step forward towards Turncoat, who recoiled so quickly that his shoulder slammed against the side of the container. After a moment, she gracefully moved back to her position on the opposite wall. "It doesn't matter what your opinions are. We don't have time to spin a world of dreams and talk. We've had years to scrutinize and theorize and subvert from the cloak of cave-shadows. If you're not ready to act, then shut up. Get out of my way. It's tonight or it never happens, ever. Then all four of us, and our friends out there, are dead anyways. And those poor wretches out there get to keep killing the planet in blissful oblivion until the rot eats them alive." She kicked away from the wall and strode with purpose towards the swung-to doors of the shipping container.

"Where are you going?" Lill called out after her.

"Where do you think?" Domina replied, pushing the doors open, battered hinges squealing and shaking rust free.

She jumped down to the ledge below. A rope ladder led up to a metal grating welded onto the side of the upper container housing their company; an improvised deck. Their housing quarter was largely shrouded under cover of total darkness, the only illumination coming from intermittent and rarely functioning cage lights.

Her bike was chained up, barely visible. An old surface bike, scrapped together but at its core a Japanese street and trail. Tough, fast, and agile enough to navigate the unwieldy organic mounds and corridors of the city as well as painted granite freeways of the megapass. It was matte black, spraypainted over patches and parts. It ran smooth, if a little loud, and never failed to start.

She adjusted her leather coat, feeling the reassuring weighty pull of her pistol beneath armored breast. She was a quick enough draw and a better aim. Lots of practice in the lower caverns and the lowest taverns of the undercity. Places the cameras didn't reach and were better off forgotten about in case questions were asked later.

"Hey, Domina," came a low rumble from the Mountain. She turned to glimpse him leaning against the open doorway of the container.

"Yeah?"

"It all ends tonight. One way or another."

"Yeah."

The Mountain nodded, bringing the bottle of homebrew to his lips, then licking them clean. His suit was spotted with missed opportunities, though any that fell on his silk tie escaped notice.

"We'll be ready," Lill called out, placing her hand on her father's hip as she appeared to say farewell.

Turncoat was nowhere to be seen.

Domina nodded her head and gave one of her wry smiles before swinging a leg over her bike. She tapped at the ignition and the chains around her axle came apart and fell loose to the dusty earth. Modification was survival, even for those up in the towers. A few vintage vestiges, concessions to style — she kickstarted the engine to life. It growled beneath her, vibrating through her bones. Pulling hard at the throttle, she pulled away from the trashheap, the conical headlights casting strange shadows over the derelict shipboxes. Dark smoke blasted from her rattling metal pipes, drilled and ported. The air got worse every year but nobody particularly noticed; it swept through great mineshafts and labyrinth passages before expelling out onto the surface. A surface that was ruined, on the balancing point of becoming hostile to all things living. Strange beasts and demons were said to stalk the scarred surface. Domina would see for herself.

Through spraypainted side streets, Domina sliced through the night.

A revved-up, screaming scalpel.

BOOK 2:

THE PAST

CHAPTER 4: THE PARTY

Simon hadn't slept in three weeks. He questioned his own sanity in brief inner monologues. At first the ruminations had been like religious screeds, taking place inside of his skull and muttered between his thin, cracked lips. He kept licking at them, feeling the roughness of them on his tongue, but it did little to moisten them. His mouth was desert dry.

He'd managed the first two weeks by expending his remaining vacation time, feigning aches and pains and illness in the midst to lengthen the time he could spend alone. The very thought of returning to the science department gave him thrills of lurching panic that he spent hours trying to control and come down from.

Simon was a meteorologist and a biologist amongst many other things. He was getting old, gray creeping into his uneven moustache and unkempt hair, which was thinning and receding away from a high and age-spotted brow. It had been many years since he'd felt the warmth of a woman in his bed, and as he looked at himself this morning, he could see why. His physique had drooped from it's less than impressive pique. His mind had apparently done the same. He could not stop his fingers from trembling no matter how many pills he downed.

His shunt wasn't functioning. A misfire here or there happened to everyone. Feedback sickness could force a recalibration. Total failure, however, meant reconditioning. It had been something he'd laughed madly about during the first few days, hopping about and whistling through his teeth. Reconditioning — a word that he and his colleagues used so casually as if to obscure the truth of what it meant.

What it meant was essentially death, a stripping, a removal, a moulding, a casting, a transplant. It was a forgery, like the old stories about a mind in a computer, or life after death. Philosophical intrigues — existential examinations — paling and peeling away in the face of his reality.

Simon was a coward — he knew this to be true of himself — and he was going to die. He knew it, and without the shunt to carry away these facts into nothingness, they stood imperiously in front of him. When he closed his eyes, a mental portrait drew itself out of lines in the black, the figments of his demise.

He left his small, messy apartment in a nondescript neighbourhood, climbed into his vehicle, and sat. He took a deep breath, still shuddering.

"Get a grip get a grip get a grip get a grip," he murmured to himself, chanting.

He fitted the keys to ignition and rolled over the engine, then pulled away from the curb. The traffic this late was always light. The majority of workers crammed in their makeshift living rooms or tumbledown taverns to watch the evening's entertainment. Elite Channel was the only show in town; Simon's work on climate and meteorology was often used to augment the humidity or atmospheric reports. Weather systems above directly influenced conditions in the cavern. Without Simon, Tatiana had stepped in to fill his place. Young, ambitious, and almost as skilled at prediction and analysis as he was, he admired the girl without desire. Age and the fact that he could see her manipulating the strings leading to his early retirement and her promotion both contributed to this apathy.

As he swung onto the megapass, Simon made an active effort to keep his train of thought away from his current condition. He noted the specks of white moving along the cavern ceiling, the coal worms hard at work. A dazzling display of fireworks arced and flashed and burst over the recreational strip to his left. Blues, reds, pinks, purples, and greens struck out like stars, cinders and ash coating the rooftops. Simon couldn't recall what holiday it was. The days had blended together, dates slipping into meaningless and arbitrary figures on the screen of his phone, his screen.

It was a short drive to work. Prime University stood a monument, second largest building in Cavern next to the Spire of the Elite. Squat, square, almost ancient in its architectural sense, the university was the seat of all knowledge remaining. Mostly stone with little glass facing outwards, it seemed a stronghold more than an academy. Seeing the vast structure always made Simon feel a bit small inside. Today, it made Simon feel very sick to his stomach. He found his parking spot in a small, sheltered parkade nestled up to the left of the front entrance of the campus.

It took him the usual fifteen minutes to reach his small and cluttered office. In through the massive main doors — all original glass, no salvaged — and into one of six primary elevators. Floor five. Five-forty-eight. He no longer had to share his 8x10 with another researcher due to his seniority, but it still stank of old coffee and mould. The wiring remained exposed above, hanging down like vines from a trellis, despite a long overdue work order.

He cleared some old books that were piled up on his chair and sat them aside before pressing the power buttons on his computer and screen. Fans whirred to life, shaking dust free. The low hum of the computer was a small comfort to Simon. He was sweating, his fingers gripping and then loosening on the armrests of his chair, molars slowly grinding.

The desktop appeared, icons and apps filling the display. Like the hardware, the software of the old times had also been scavenged and adapted — even ancient books gave some insight as to the logical apparatus behind the graphical shell. Human intuition also remained an uncanny constant, and lines of thought allowed what *was* to *become* once again. A tropical beach filled the twenty seven inches of

49

high def. It was a dream to Simon and all of his people, as fantastic as dragons. In this dark world, demons murdered mutants and each other on a barren and blasted surface.

He had seen the demons and dismissed them before, his concerns carried away. Without the shunt, he felt the *pain* of the palm trees, blue water, a sun naked to the eye — realities carried into the future by this image that would never be again — Simon caught himself on the verge of tears again and quickly wiped at his nose and shook his head.

Such things were his passion and despite his many flaws, the ones he counted and etched on the inside of his flesh to remind himself of his lack of worth, he knew that he was a sensitive. A dreamer. Days beyond ominous clouds and acid rain and the constant damp.

Texts arrived. Hundreds. Advertisements from his usual haunts constituting about half — coupons, discounts, loyalty cards. The majority of the rest routine forwards — journal excerpts, citations, corrections. One was marked urgent, flashing a bright cyan against the black of the monitor.

INVITATION — SCIENCE AND TECHNOLOGY GALA — RSVP — MAND.

It was the MAND that struck Simon. He'd had access to his email accounts from his home network but not to internal memos. He read the letter.

FROM: dtermin@uprime.intra

*TO: *@sci.uprime.intra*

This is a reminder to all faculty (including adjuncts and contract lecturers) that the annual SCIENCE AND TECHNOLOGY GALA will be taking place this evening, in The Estuary. Formalwear required. All department heads and research leads will need to deliver a short speech. As always, it's going to be a great deal of fun!

Attendance is mandatory; sick notes or excuses unacceptable.

Yours,

Dr. Danitha Termin

Ph.D, Biology and Genetics

That had been his morning.

Now Simon was seated at the gala, sweating even more profusely and attempting, in vain, to drown his nerves in an alcoholic ocean.

The great room, The Estuary, capitalized because it was a dining establishment now rather than the simple brook and pool it had been in earlier days. Though like those earlier days, a thick and loamy moss still coated the walls like climbing ivy. A dark and earthy scent, mushrooms and cold water, was blown gently about the room by small and unobtrusive fans. Audible, a gentle sound, the movement of the water. The natural granite of the cavern was carved lovingly, complimented by ornate sculptures – mythical beasts found in books from beyond the beginning beside novel imaginings by new artists.

Two hundred large, circular tables were sprawled across the great hall that had been built in the basement of the university for formal occasions. They were topped with fine white linen cloth and crimson table runners emblazoned with the logo of Prime University in golden thread. Centerpieces of fresh fruit, cultivated in the hydroponics caves below their primary cavern, were placed evenly, for appearances – until after the formalities at least.

Simon was seated with his colleagues. To his left, Dr. Inine, a strawberry-haired and frail gentleman who spoke with a lisp. He was their coder. To his right, Dr. Hoka. She was tall, muscular, and intimidating – she often sneered while speaking, giving off a cynical, critical impression. Simon felt that this was not altogether uncommon amongst academics; he had often found himself resorting to the same browbeating body language.

Others spread out along the table, including the department director, Dr. Lear. A small, petite woman of a dusky peach complexion, her placid demeanour obscured razor sharp wit and tongue. She was well respected and well liked by nearly all of the meteorology department with the exception of a few perennial malcontents.

The wine was white, a Riesling that had originated in what had once been the lush vineyards of Germany. Data gathered from the few remaining satellites which passed overhead showed that most of Europe was scorched and barren. Nothing was left standing. The genetics of this German grape survived. Riesling vines thrived in the agricultural caverns, borne to tart sweetness that exploded on his palate and obscured the alcohol which coursed through his veins.

Simon smiled. He felt happy for the first time in

months. Since the first time he'd had to hide the secret of his broken shunt.

The thought returned to his mind and his smile faded; now the dark tide of drink turned against him as quickly as it had bolstered his spirit, his soul, not a moment before. His inner struggles must have played out on his face, as Dr. Hoka cut into his rumination.

"Hey, Dr. Dools. You okay over there? Maybe you'd best lay off the wine for a bit," and there, the characteristic sneer. This time it brought a flush of anger to his cheeks.

"Dr. Hoka," he said, inclining his head and raising his glass smoothly in toast. "To your empathy and kindness, which all so deeply acknowledge and appreciate."

A few other attendees at the table had caught the exchange and chuckled, some hiding their faces behind well manicured nails or napkins. Dr. Hoka's proud face darkened, the edges of her lips turning downward. She'd not expected the worm to show a spine.

Simon kept and caught her gaze, then tilted the crystal to his lips and drank deeply. The sweet wine was refreshing and invigorating. He caught Hoka's eyes trailing his glass, seeing he had nearly drained it.

He wagged a finger and comically admonished her.

"Now now, Doctor. Eyes on your own glass, please. Wouldn't want anyone to get the wrong impression," completed with a wry smile and a twinkle of mischief in his eye, Simon delivered the verbal coup de gras.

The tittering turned to outright laughter as the table could not contain themselves any longer. Ladies leaned back in their chairs, painted lips parted; gentlemen pounded the table roughly and rattled the crystal and silverware, looking at one another with wicked smiles.

Hoka ground her teeth, her jaw muscles visibly moving, bulging up around her jawline. Her eyes were like a wounded predator, locked on the drunken shine emitted by Dr. Simon Dools as he lazed, one arm over the back of his chair, mocking her attacks.

The battle was interrupted by the sound of speech pouring forth from the speaker system aligned in surround about the estuary. Clear, crisp tones that bespoke an aristocratic, Elite upbringing gushed forth to greet those assembled for the annual soiree.

"Welcome, welcome, please."

The clamour eroded to the sconced edges of the estuary. Even then, it was a low murmurs and hushed whispers.

The mistress of ceremonies continued, splendid in her elaborate fabric gown. Bright swatches of peacock fabric reached up to grace the contour of her breast and neck, sweeping about her shoulders in elaborate curls. Firey down, burnt phoenix, crumbled into cinder and ash upon her shoulders in the form of a silken shrug, translucent and stitched with LED emitters. Her name was Alana Hellwig; she was a professor emeritus of electrical engineering and spokeswoman for the scientific arts of Prime University.

Couture, the height of reserved high culture. She spoke with a steely timbre and a vast intelligence. All listened, hanging on her every word.

"Tonight we come together to celebrate famous – and *infamous* – figures in the pursuit of our knowledge, the scientific exploration of what there is to be known for the betterment of our lives!"

To this, madam speaker was greeted with polite and growing applause.

"As you all know this year has been pivotal for Prime University. We have long stood as the font of information, technology, and entertainment that has served all of us so dearly in these last few years of gloom and darkness. We have all felt the effects at one time or another – an instant of doubt, a snatched memory that seems to unnerve you, something misremembered."

The applause died and expressions turned to stone as each searched themselves for the truth that they were hearing.

"Now our research has forestalled doom and disaster. As scientists and researchers, the best of all amongst our colleagues, we worked together to achieve something very important. The data we've gathered has been of unparallelled importance to the high Elite. The Watcher has told us that the reports from our biology department correlates with his own data; he has passed along to me that plans are being made as we speak to ensure a painless transition into our next generation. Ladies and gentlemen, what I am telling you is – it's not going to be like last time."

Drunken ebullience erupted, even the normally quiet joining in good cheer. The last time a transition between catalysts had been made, it had been a hasty affair with less than two weeks' warning. On such short notice, many shunts with weakened batteries or malfunctions had led to disasters, horrific scenes of perversion and violence that still conjured up memories to rail against amongst many in the audience. Filmclips and fear stoked bonfires in their hearts, egos bolstered by booze and flattery.

"We are prepared. Prepared in so many ways. Our technology department has implemented new control systems over the ductwork fans that mean we can increase emissions by fifty percent over the next five years. Cleaner air and less moisture and dampness overall. Dr. Ingvall in Chemistry reports that the new compound they've been testing — we call it "surface serum" and some of you may have heard it mentioned in the most recent journal — is a resounding success. It has taken years of painstaking longitudinal datamining, cross-examination, and labwork that has culminated in this achievement. No longer will we lose fine men and women to the walking sin that plagues the surface!"

Her voice here was nearly hysterical; it was a well known fact that Dr. Hellwig had lost her husband, the principal researcher on an ill-fated surface team, just years ago. The fact seemed even more poignant, pulling at them, drawing the audience in, hanging on her words. Even Simon felt himself taking his eyes from the rim of his Reisling to pay closer attention to the epic speech.

"And last, but certainly not least, our meteorology and climate science staff." Dr. Hellwig paused a moment, inclining her head towards the table at which Simon was seated. "Without the analysis provided by our team while analyzing the data recovered from surface expeditions, we wouldn't have what is the most encouraging discovery of the year. Perhaps the last few years — arguably an entire generation."

Simon squirmed in his seat, removing his hands from the tabletop and shifting them to his lap. The spotlights swung to grace their table, illuminating them as shining spectacle. He began to feel hot and a little nauseous.

"Doctors Hoka, Dools, Haverford, Gnemmi, Bello, Inine, and department head Lear, I present you all to the audience for your due reward. Please stand."

Steepling his fingers against the table for support, Simon gained a shaky stance, bobbing his head in an approximation of acknowledgment. Hoka beamed, a wide grin splitting her face. Lear remained impassive, while Inine raised a hand to wave, turning about to take in the rippling applause. Gnemmi and Bello were copiously drunk and leaned on one another, raising their glasses in toast to the estuary, spilling only a little wine on the carpet. Haverford looked almost as uncomfortable as Simon, a hulk of a man fit into a suit two sizes two small; he stood awkwardly as a rose blush bloomed in his already ruddy cheeks.

"… if it were not for the determinations made by the models and consultations provided by these fine men and women, we would not be sure. Sure of the secret I am about to reveal to all of you, something that we will share with the rest very soon," Dr. Hellwig continued.

The esteemed elder doctor paused a moment for dramatic effect, curling her fingers about the lip of the podium and leaning forward conspiratorially.

"The weather warms. The snow melts. Our summers will

grow longer. The bad rain will move away in a matter of years, not a matter of lifetimes. We can divert the massive amount of power we use to cycle the wastewater to enhancing our lives, our security, our happiness. The surface dwellers dwindle in numbers; we have seen them slay each other indiscriminately but, as time goes on, their strength flags."

Dr. Hellwig gave the audience a moment to reflect, on her words. She felt the radiating waves of relief and calm and joy that were refracted back to her from the personalities at play in the room and was visibly pleased.

"In short, esteemed colleagues... we can stay exactly where we are, without fear, for the perceivable future. Our home is safe."

Now thunder pealed as hands clapped together and throaty voices husky with emotion came forth from the gallery and the floor, enough to shack the slabstone foundations of the university. Crystal and silver rattled, clinking together on the tables, some guests percussively tapping them together. Simon felt sick to his stomach, the truth twisting inside of him, contrary and seething to the surface. The booze helped to bring it down, but he started to feel an uncomfortable heat in his head.

The thunder died out, some tipsy scholars falling heavily back into their seats or out of them entirely. Pockets of laughter were suppressed at the sight; Dr. Hellwig smiled at these softly, saying –

"Now then. Now then. Secure in the knowledge that we can sleep night after night without the whine of the shunt so loud in our minds, shall we not celebrate? Dinner is served; we will have the formal research awards for individuals after dessert. Thank you all, and please do enjoy."

With this, the mistress of ceremonies swept from the podium with practiced grace. The organic lines of her gown took on new dimensions from every angle, and so most continued to watch as she moved along the stage, down the stairs, and began to circulate amongst those who'd come to this evening's gala. Smiling, shaking hands, exchanging laughter and conversation – Dr. Hellwig was renowned for her ability to work a room. Part of the reason she had been selected by the high Elite and why she had retained her post for so long despite great competition.

Simon was almost exclusively focused on trying to stoke an appetite for the dinners that were now being carted out by catering staff. Silverplated buffet wagons took up positions on the irregular edges of the estuary chamber, finding space wherever they might fit. Harried white-gloved hands snatched plates free, scooped food, ladled sauces. Delicious mounds of whipped potatoes, a thin line of pure butter running down the midst, nestled about bits of fresh corn. Succulent spiced chicken breast, marinated in chives and broth, a luxury rarely afforded even the wealthiest citizens of the city beneath the surface. Despite his drunkenness and his shattered nerves, the aroma wafting forth from the plate that was set in front of him was enough to dispel any hesitation about eating.

The food was divine; Simon had never had anything better. The wine paired with the pleasure of his palate as the butter and salt and fat slid over his tongue. It was almost enough to distract him from the congratulatory backslapping and excitable chatter which he knew to be complete lies. Salt turned to ash in his mouth.

"It's not true," he murmured to his plate, hoping nobody would hear.

Hoka, who had been feigning interest in conversation with one of the other scientists, broke off conversation politely and turned to Simon. The tug at the corner of her lips returned.

"Simon, were you saying something? You've been pretty quiet since the meal started and I thought I saw you saying something over there. We know you're not the most religious man so I know they're not prayers!" she laughed scornfully. Others began to pay attention, again anticipating a show.

"I said that she didn't tell the whole story, as we all know. I don't mean to sour the mood of the evening, I was just..."

"Just what?" Hoka snorted incredulously, eyes alight. "Dr. Dools, you know very well that your pet theory about the increasing rain and the rising tides has not borne any weight with more serious scholars."

There it was, the barb. He dodged it, despite the drink in his stomach pushing him towards rage – the ultimate taboo in polite society, particularly here in the heart of the academy. The insult was commonplace enough, though, and so as his face flushed scarlet it brought the expected tittering rather than the shock that would have been shown if he revealed his true self, clawing itself free of his throat.

"Just this. It's true that the bad rain — acidic rain — will diminish in the years to come if the long-term data we recovered from the surface card is to be believed. But, what about the increasing instability that the ancients warned of? The tides have indeed risen. The Huntress herself has said as much to us."

Dr. Gnemmi took a break from leaning on Dr. Bello to respond, her voice thick. "Oh give it a rest, Simon! We've heard this all before! Can't you just be happy? Are you nuts? We're being treated like royalty here!"

"... And the six months of snow every year?" Simon pressed on, ignoring her. "Within the span of a generation? If we don't prepare, we'll be without any means to propagate, to advance. It will be a disaster. Doom, almost certainly."

"We always knew you were a depressing sort Simon, but

this? Doomsayer is a poor way to moonlight when you're an academy researcher. You should know better than to believe in this nonsense, this mysticism."

"Your minds are clouded by drink and self-righteousness."

"Look who's talking!" Hoka sneered, this time the point scored and the table joined in mean laughter. It was shortlived.

"Well, don't stop on my account!" Dr. Hellwig said, having arrived tableside, laying a hand on the back of chairs belonging to Gnemmi and Bello. "What's the joke?"

"Nothing, Dr. Hellwig," Simon tried, smoothly. Under the carpet to save face.

"Oh come now! Don't be shy, I can handle a rude one now and then."

"Dr. Dools was just saying that he does not necessarily agree with what you were saying earlier," Dr. Hoka said. He wasn't getting away that easily. Eyes widened amongst those assembled. Shock spread over the spokeswoman's face.

"Dr. Dools. While your colleagues may find a rakish lack

of respect for the facts to be funny, I can assure you that I do not," the amicability displayed mere seconds ago by Dr. Hellwig had burned off, evaporated.

Simon struggled to find his voice, his confidence fleeting.

"I, I... really, Dr. Hellwig, it's not like that. They're misrepresenting me. Putting words in my mouth," he stammered.

"What a weasel!" Bello boomed. "Just five minutes ago he was saying that you are glossing over the evidence, failing to acknowledge the facts of the future."

"What future? Oh yes!" the spokeswoman feigned revelation. "The floods. Rising tides. Migrating mutant populations. Disease vectors. Oh, and aren't we immunosuppressed from lack of surface exposure? I forgot, Dr. Dools, about your pet conspiracies. I thought you'd grown out of them, to be honest."

And now, gales of laughter as one and all realized how the lines had been drawn.

"You'll excuse me," Simon muttered darkly, buttoning his suit jacket and pushing his chair back from the table.

The jeers trailed him all the way to the door. He felt like he would be sick at any moment; his suit jacket felt wet and clammy, there was fire in his head and wetness threatened his eyes. If he'd stayed, he would have instantly revealed himself. As it was, they took his snub as wounded pride; something every academic – shunted or not – was familiar with.

"Tired of being their damn whipping boy," Simon growled to himself as he stalked up the stairwell leading to the exit level. "Not going to take this crap anymore. Not." He beat his fist against his thin, frail chest as if hoping to impress someone who was not there, or perhaps himself. The pain stayed with him for a few moments. It made him feel better.

The drunkenness made the walk back to his studio dwelling seem shorter and more pleasant than it had been in the past. He took the time to admire the architecture of his neighbourhood, butting up on the eastern edge of campus. One of the few clusters approved for non-greenhouse foliage, a few simple bushes and trees were treats for the senses. Even at this hour, lovers sat beside them on blankets and looked longingly at the break of the branches, the emerald of healthy buds. He watched them as he walked, closing his eyes and imagining them against the bright blue sky of the surface, backlit by the sun. These solitary trees planted in the cavern deeps and illuminated by a false light were impressions and imitations of nature. He took a superficial joy in them, far removed.

He was tired of illusions, sick to death of pretense. Exhausted by his own pretending, he was reaching the end of his rope. The drink wore off as he crossed the threshold into his apartment, feeling leaden and stupid and ashamed. He wished for the shunt again and knew that now it would be impossible without total recalibration. How much of himself would be lost in the process? The assurances of the academy, the elite, the institutions that governed his life were as empty as the speech he'd heard tonight.

And Simon knew why. Their shunts were functioning properly. They saw the forest without seeing the trees. This forest was blighted, and yet the machinery in their minds would only allow them to feel, to grasp, those few trees that remained vital. They were addicted to ignorance and bliss, intoxicated. Danger did not exist for them, only the moment, and the moment was always wondrous. Drugs, tradition, routine, and endless entertainment were the milieu, technologically enhanced — and enforced.

He'd slipped the net. The sleeper had awoken. He knew now that his earlier thoughts of subtlety, of trying to reintegrate into the collective he now understood to be living under a spell, a grand illusion, were misguided.

The data told the whole story and they were only willing to hear the half of it that pleased them, that made them feel good, that warmed their insides. The other half tore the good news to shreds — without preparation and drastic change, in fact, exodus from the cavern within the next generation or so — they were all dead. No future for anyone. Laughter and jollity until the very last cup, drowning while oblivious to the fact. That was their vision of the future, dead and hollow behind a paper mask. Not his. His vision was born of a shaman's mask, dense foliage, organic. Born of a nightmare he'd been having every evening for weeks.

Simon locked his door, feeling the deadbolt slam home. He took all of his tech and bundled it up in a messenger bag. Every datastick, optical disc, cloud address and password, and tablet. His untidy little home looked the same as it always did, barring the holes where longstanding articles of clothing or gear had rested. Old books fell into impromptu piles at random on the floor and on the countertops. Clothes were strewn about recklessly, mostly black but with a few reds mixed in. Old salvaged posters depicting long-dead celebrities hung in simple frames from the walls; a pity he'd not be able to take those with him.

There simply wasn't time. Psych evaluation would almost certainly be arranged as soon as possible, perhaps even as early as tomorrow morning. Dr. Hoka, gunning for the end of his career or his life (whichever came first), would ensure it. She was a favorite of Dr. Hellwig's and that favour ran very deeply.

This is why Simon had to leave tonight, before the crack of dawn. He needed to disappear. Shouldering his black labcoat and turning his collar to the cold, Dr. Dools died and a shadow crept into the furthest nooks and crannies of the cavern, lying patiently in wait. Opportunity came calling shortly thereafter, wearing a blood red robe and riding a battered motorcycle.

CHAPTER 5: LILL'S LAST FEW MONTHS

A month ago, Lill saw her father in the flesh for the first time in years. They were standing under the garish glow of the exit sign just outside of the back door of a container bar, The Moon — one of any number of "safe" drinking holes. A shunt scan was constantly in effect at the door, signaling patrons whenever anyone entered who was "active." Tonight, however, luck had afforded them the grace to have never heard the alarm, not even when The Mountain had crossed the threshold. He'd come stumbling in, almost drunkenly, still a bit overwhelmed. He had been bruised and beaten and confused.

In the end, it had all been worth it.

That night had started with an agonizing conversation between her and Domina. She'd been hiding a secret for months during her second year at Cavern City University (Primary Campus) and she felt like she couldn't hide anything else any longer. So she told Domina what happened.

Lill was a good student; money was never a concern for her given her full academic scholarship, let alone the fact that her father was a famous fighter. Well, *used to be* famous.

Her first year had been exemplary; she'd made the very top percentile of the Dean's list, double majoring in software theory and theosophy. It was the latter path of study which led her to the secret that would change her life forever.

She had been jacked in to her home terminal, the padded visor over her eyes, her vision filled with text and hypertext, images, sounds, 3D environments. Her research demanded a keen mind and the ability to multitask for hours on end, downing cup after cup of loose tea and the odd drug-infused drink. Her apartment was tidy to a fault, as orderly and perfect as her mind, though minimalist. A small oaken endtable rested by the bed, holding up a simple vase bearing white lilies. Above it, a framed photograph of her and her dad, before the bad times. Before he started losing.

She rarely thought of him, and if she did, such thoughts were whisked away as if they'd never been. The picture was the only thing in her apartment bearing a film of dust.

It was a spartan and efficient 150 square feet. No carpeting, white ceiling and floors with walls a rich rose. Vinyl art clung to the walls in places, nothing overwrought, simply slopes and lines, never intersecting, often asymmetrical, always black. Her single bed was built upon a retractable shelf; she kept her clothing suspended above and her footwear below. There were over a thousand such compartments in this building alone, the entire campus residence hub was comprised of 18 such buildings in total. Only the best were admitted to residence; the mediocre students were forced onto tube transit or a lengthy commute.

Then, amongst the innumerable glowing windows that crowded her visored vision as she sat online, she got the message.

It was going to happen tonight. The rescue effort. To reclaim her dad.

After they'd had their argument, and it had been decided that they were going to reclaim The Mountain, Lill had climbed onto the back of Domina's bike after dressing down to go out, clinging to the leatherclad back of the far larger woman. A hardwired link between their two helmets allowed them to speak to one another despite the maddening noise of the megapass, a tiny and nearly invisible tether. Twenty lanes at the widest, winding about the enormous cavern system like an ancient amusement park ride, the megapass was congested at the best of times. The smoke and fumes were almost choking as they rose upward, caught by enormous industrial fans mounted to the stone ceiling, some to the more solid stalactites. Unlucky "coal worms," usually unrepentant or unbreakable Flawed, were sent to the surface through these airways. Sent to repair a solar panel array or to scavenge for materials, many coal worms never came back, though most did. Domina could see one now, his trademark white suit standing out against the darkness of the cavern ceiling, scaling the fan mounts and beginning his ascent. Bearing a childhood fear of heights, Domina couldn't repress a shudder at the thought. Lill felt this and gripped her bodyguard even tighter.

"You're sure that he's going to be there tonight, right? This is a one-shot opportunity, too high profile of a target and too little time to try this again," Domina said, her voice crackling to life in Lill's helmet.

"Yes. I saw the social media event page and all of the comments indicate that it's on."

"Good." A beat. "You nervous?" She asked her rider.

The traffic flow accelerated around them. Low-slung small vehicles sped by, many bearing a few improvised parts and only a few the glossy black or red that denoted status.

"I-I think so. I feel strange. Almost ill. My stomach..." She almost felt like vomiting. Lill gritted her teeth and remained silent.

"You're nervous. It's normal. Hell, I'm nervous and I'm used to this shit."

"Not for me it isn't. Not normal, I mean," Lill said quietly.

Lill had only been flawed for a matter of months; what had begun as a frightening secret and a struggle to maintain face in public had become gnawing, doing damage over time as she acclimated to life without a conduit to the catalyst. Domina, born illegally and never having had a shunt implanted, had never known perpetual peace of mind.

A large truck bearing a flat tech-illuminated ad for ESSENCE SMOKE pushed past them on the right flank — though they were hurtling at great speed the bus just couldn't keep pace. The faces, hidden behind soot and dust, stared downward, checking their devices for updates. Not a single one looked towards the window, almost entirely covered with filth from the road. The advertisement shone through the dust, the contours of the cloud of billowing smoke taking on the characteristics of paisley from the old world.

The horizon that fell open to them as they rounded the major crescent of the megapass into the surrounding area was a familiar sight to Lill; it was where most of the population of the city lived. Commerce and elite business took place in the core. To the rest fell the small spaces and compact existences, the positive externalities of a flawless life free from want. Since Lill had read that phrase in the book, that illusion provided by the neural-narcotic power of the shunt had melted away around her, immaterial and insubstantial. Beyond reason.

Lill had not known reason before she'd read *the book*.

She'd been digging through the stacks at the library. The old style archives, those dusty floors atop the low slung concrete building they call the library, although the majority of students prefer the interactive portal. Lill had always loved and appreciated the smell of books, the spicy scent of the pages, the mystique of the hands that had bent the pages before. Again, immaterial – but this time with love.

Her fingers had traced along the spine of this particular tome with love, appreciating it's fine leatherbound texture. It had been hidden to her in previous examinations, buried behind an obscure tome on Italian and French fusion cooking that had been intriguing but useless.

It was a book with no title. Bound in a simple black leather, pebbled and worn by the touch of countless and unknowable hands.

She had never seen a book with no name. She opened the book and confronted an unsettling picture, a man and woman intertwined, sitting nude. Vulnerable, their flesh obviously exposed, the folds of their flesh hanging loose. One arm each had around the other, clinging tight. Their heads en passent, cradled on each others shoulder. The other hand was outstretched, fingers splayed.

There was an image of pain, longing. Pretense and faith. Beneath them, written by hand, in an uneducated scrawl.

"Life is pain. I have lost much in my life. So have you. We *endure* together. We are *extinguished* alone."

Below this in a shaking yet elegant hand:

"To be human is to suffer. Live again."

And then, as if literally grasped by the hand of God and shaken, Lill felt something move through her. She contorted, dropping the book with an abrupt noise that may have startled anyone nearby if any had been about, then clawed at her skull.

She writhed and gritted her teeth as unfamiliar and unpleasant feelings flooded her. The shunt, she realized in a state of panick, was not working! Her fingers found the cool metal of the port buried into her body. It was in vain; the pain continued.

Hours later, covered in sweat and shivering, Lill was finally able to crawl out of the shower and lay in bed, sleeping for a full day and missing her classes. Alert e-mails and instant messages pinged into her inbox, their tonal arrival the punctuation that dotted her unusual slumber, not awake and yet not fully under.

As she slept she had visions. Her life, contorted. Her spotless academic record stained by feedback sickness. Images of the catalyst, the Sufferer. The ache of her own hurt. The stern and aging face of her father, increasingly grizzled and at times unrecognizable to her, defeated. Again and again in front of her, knocked to the ground, a dead pile of flesh.

She'd felt powerless and alone. She'd called her father and received, as always, his voicebox. So she'd hid her secret. For months. Until she couldn't take it anymore and rode the transit tubes down to the trasheaps under the megapass. Under the guise of field research.

Even atop the megapass, their bike screaming downslope into the outskirts of the city core, she could see the fringes of the folk settlements that sprung from underneath. Metal scraps, street signs, rubber hose, tarpaulins, plastic wrap and other debris collected from above was distributed through the proper channels until the absolute waste was given up for public offering. Thousands upon thousands of desperate hands grabbed for gems in the pile.

Nonetheless, while the shunt was active, even these poor ones were happy. They had shelter and the privacy of their dwellings. They had food and were able to see doctors if they felt sick. They had jobs to do that afforded them the dignity of labour. When she saw them picking through the refuse nowadays, her own shunt dead in her skull, she couldn't help but feel sorry for them, not quite able to say why. She no longer watched her father fight, and lose, either.

Except for tonight. Domina has sent her that message to her dorm room and she had known that everything was going to change.

Tonight. Lill readjusted her hold around Domina's torso, feeling the sweat of her palms seep into the leather jacket.

Traffic began to thin as they moved several short exits away from the core city. The cave walls themselves seemed to close in, the ceiling coming closer. Jagged teeth in the form of the stalactites threatened the ceilings of the few office and apartment buildings that stood in the outermost quarters.

"Thinking about him?" Domina's voice cut into her helmet.

"Yes. A little."

"A lot. Don't lie to me, Lill. I hate it."

"Okay, okay. A lot.' Lill paused. "You think we can really do it?"

Seconds passed with only the thrumming sound of the engine beneath them, droning.

"Yeah. Hell yeah," Domina said.

The leather-clad woman twisted at the handlebars and kicked down the gear, whipping the bike between two luxury cars into the nearest offramp. Looking side to side, Lill took in the scenery as the bike moaned loudly, complaining at having to be throttled, shuddering slightly underneath.

Flat buildings were built irregularly, like plates of an armored shell seeking cover under one another. A shield wall. While the cavern ceiling along the core was cut and monitored, rockfall here dented the metal rooftops, stones still sitting atop most. Illuminated storefronts peppered the winding streets, most of them advertising wine, pills, cheap refined calories. There was nothing like getting drunk without any of the nastiness. Lill had learned the hard way that drinking without a shunt led to a whole new level of agony the next day. The morning after that drunk, she'd told Turncoat to reactivate her conduit immediately. She'd only been half joking.

There were no homeless, however, and even in these small ad hoc spaces the people seemed happy. If you asked any of them, they were happy. Stained walls and canned food in the cupboards didn't make a difference to them as long as things continued as they were. Even under the strained streetlamps affixed to building corners and certain storefronts, Lill could see small groups of people – lovers, friends, business partners   strolling along the sidewalks, talking in the evening.

She envied them and pitied them; two emotions that were relatively new to her but had become intimate friends already. She'd taken up drinking and taking a few pills now and then to take the edge off. Tonight she was clean; her fear was a necessary instinct when going into such a foreign situation.

They reached the bottom of the offramp, Domina turning her battered black helmet left and right, checking for traffic. Seeing none, she gripped the accelerator and pressed the motor, jumping forward and making a left onto a short circuit towards a shopping strip.

"You need anything before we go in? Belltime is never on time," Domina said over the radio.

"Just a few things."

"Gotcha. Grotto's it is."

Domina expertly swept the bike over the median and pulled through a narrow alleyway between two stores, coming to a rest near a dumpster tucked into a corner. Grotto's was a personal favourite and a friendly place of business, named after the owner herself.

They walked down the alley, then turned onto the street, removing their helmets as they did so. This section of the strip was relatively busy; a cluster of teenage girls walked by wearing the latest spray-ons — an elderly gentleman and his wife tottered along arm in arm. There was no bustle here in the outskirts; most revelers were pressing into the core like a mad mob, leaving the less enthusiastic behind.

Entering Grotto's was like coming home for Domina, and like meeting a new friend for Lill. The store was dimly lit in comparison to the wall of illumination provided by the various shops nearby. Old fluorescent tubes flickered here and there above the beverage coolers, stocked mostly with cheap beer. The coolers themselves ran on minimal electricity to conserve power, cut deep-down into the floor like an ancient root cellar, stocked with cave ice.

Black Star, Red Line, Green Hopper — all the old favourites. Domina turned sideways, shoulder forward, winding her way between the narrow aisles towards the beer. Lill walked to the counter, a simple wooden affair that had seen so much business that the veneer itself was completely worn away. In a way, it resembled images of ancient wooden collection plates Lill had read about in the database and in the stacks; coin was a rarity nowadays but the notion remained the same.

"Need a box of Noviprexx and two bottles of Lift, please," Lill said to the clerk, a young woman with peacock plumed hair and a somewhat studied, bored expression. The clerk must have had a lot of practice killing time in a dive like this.

The clerk nodded, shrugging off the counter, crouching down behind and fumbling at the makeshift pharmacy box they kept there. Noviprexx tablets were expensive, single-serve, and helped to calm the nerves. Lift on the other hand was quite the stimulant, sold in liquid formate, injected with chemicals to produce mental alertness and quickened reflexes. A little bit of light rustling later, and she popped back up with the drugs in hand.

By now Domina had returned from the beverage cooler, a case of Black Star in tow. She set it down on the countertop beside Lill's purchase.

"Don't worry Lill. I got it." Domina tossed a disposable credit card onto the countertop. "Should cover it. Tip the rest."

"Sure thing," the clerk said. "You know... you really shouldn't mix all that, right?"

"Right."

Domina smiled in reply, picked up the beer, and headed for the door. Lill snatched her items from the countertop and scrambled to catch up.

They continued back down the alleyway until they wound around the corner where the bike was resting. Domina set the case of beer down on the concrete and cracked it open.

"Won't fit on the bike unless we break it down into bags."

Domina unzipped one of the vertical pockets streaked across her leather jacket and pulled out a handful of opaque plastic bags from various shops. She started putting the bottles into the bags, two or three each, wrapping the plastic around to reduce noise and the chance of breakage. She snatched the last two from the box, and tossed one to Lill.

"Catch."

Lill dropped her bags and awkwardly reached out to catch the beer, palming it almost by fluke, feeling her fingers wrapped around the cold glass. The label was sweaty and moist in her hand.

"Nice!" Domina laughed, doubling over. "No way in hell I thought you would catch that one!"

Domina leaned with her back against the bricks, next to the dumpster. The coarse surface gripped at the leather of her jacket and added yet more age. She reached a hand into an inner pocket for her makings, pulling a zip of dark herbs and papers loose. She started to roll herself a smoke, holding the beer between her thighs.

Lill sipped at hers, feeling the cold bite run across her lips and tongue and down her throat. It hit her stomach in slight protest, but stayed put. She took a longer sip.

"You think Turncoat is right about this? I mean, the world above?"

Domina did not reply immediately, her eyes squinted slightly as she worked her fingers in the near perfect dark. She brought the smoke to her lips and licked the gumline, rolling it shut.

"Yeah. Hasn't been wrong so far."

"Isn't that a good reason to say to hell with it and re-shunt?"

"No future's that grim."

Lill raised an eyebrow.

"Really? I'm not so sure, myself."

A pause.

"I mean... *knowing* is important to me. But..." Lill continued, then again trailed off.

Another pause.

"Is it worth it? Ignorance was easier. Ironically more fulfilling."

Domina spat violently, then took a hard pull of her own beer, wiping her lips clean with her leather sleeve.

"Easier? Illusions and fantasies are easy. Life is hard. Fulfilling? Perhaps."

"What's the point in doing things the hard way?"

"Self-respect. Knowledge of personal endurance. Shared suffering, together, even if everyone is apart. Joy is nothing if it's entirely artificial. Fake. Most importantly, a lie. I want life, not a damn dream. A dream that would kill all of us. "

Domina delivered all this flatly, without hyperbole. A

leering smile stole over her expression.

"Plus, beer tastes better when you have sins to drown."

Lill laughed at this, caught off-guard by a bit of comedy to break the tension. Domina had already become so close to her; Lill looked up to the leather-clad heroine in her blood and black colours.

"Never looked at it that way. Just liked to get drunk for the feeling. No hangover, felt great."

"And a few hundred kids die every year on operating tables with pumps down into their guts. The pain teaches you a lesson, a way of telling you enough is enough."

Lill shrugged, defensively.

"I didn't care; none of us did. The party must go on. The laser-lights, the bodies next to you on the dance floor, the rows of powders and pills. It's still hard for me to understand that side of me. It's like getting to know a whole new person, and that person is *yourself*."

"Always knew who I was. But I understand," Domina said. Her beer was half empty in her hand.

"Looking outward rather than inward scares me," Lill

said.

Domina barked a laugh. "That doesn't surprise me — take a look around at this place. Even the nicest and slickest buildings in city center are covered in smoke. You could drill a thousand damn vents to the surface and it wouldn't be enough."

"That's not really what I meant, but... what do you mean? You mean we can't stay here?"

Domina shook her head, negative. "Not if you believe what Turncoat tells me. With evidence to back it up. Before he defected; back when he was a sysadmin for the Elites and the city government."

Lill's eyes widened. "How long can we stay here? I mean at the most."

"Turncoat's numbers from the meteorological and climate charts show that this area of the continent has seen very little rain over the past few centuries for a few reasons. As everyone knows, we've started seeing some leaks, even into the main chamber here. I'm not a scientist so I can't explain it to you. He can. Basically we're in for a lot more rain, and the rain will be a great deal more corrosive in nature than what we're used to."

"Floods?"

"Floods, damage to our old power and data lines running to the panels on the surface. They already seem to be throwing as many coal worms up those shafts as they can round up from between the cracks, and it's still not enough — and we're not even facing the ramp up to crisis yet."

Lill shuddered, shaking her head and beginning to pace.

"Lill." She felt a strong hand on her shoulder. Looked over to see Domina looking down at her, smiling. "This is why we're doing all this. If these people don't wake up, they'll all die. Everyone."

Lill stiffened and fought down a surge of tears. Inexperienced as she was, her wall broke. She cried softly. Domina held her tight. For a few moments, and then a few more. The night air, even on the cavern floor, was crisp and cool and only slightly damp to match the trail on Lill's cheeks. She wiped them clean and smiled up weakly at her new and closest friend.

"Sorry Domina." Lill sniffed a bit.

"Hey." Domina held the smaller girl out at arms length. "Don't ever apologize for being brave enough to show your wounds. That's what we're fighting for. It doesn't have to be that way. We can save a lot of lives. We're going to start with your dad."

Lill's weak smile improved into a wider one.

"Now let's finish this damn beer and get on with it!" Domina called out, tilting the bottle to her lips, striding back towards the Yamaha.

She sat astride and fitted her helmet, mirror shades across the front. Lill followed suit and resumed her position pressed into the larger woman's back. Domina walked the bike back a bit before kicking it up and pushing out from the alleyway back into the marketplace street.

It wasn't much of a drive to the squat saltbox housing the fights tonight, garishly decorated with bright bunting that had seen better days.

The parking lot adjacent was about three quarters full. Most of the parked vehicles were wrecks, strung together with wire and found materials without any of the ingenuity or elegance that her bike exhibited. Rusted trucks with wooden bumpers and scrapmetal beds were cast about in heaps. Balsa wood and tin sportsters with hot engines were likely to go up in a blaze while punching it down the strip.

She could already imagine the crowd huddled around the cage inside, sprawled out in uneven waves, irregular rings. Moving and weaving between each other, passing drinks and catcalls and bets, the electric tension before blood was to be spilled moving through them all like a drug.

Domina knew the addiction got even more devilish after you shut off the shunt. Pain became real and manifold. It was the lowest low on its face and the highest high on the dark side.

Every single individual lived in a fantastically fast lane. Embrace the filth, revel in it. Domina could sympathize; anyone could.

Poor bastards don't even appreciate it. Domina smiled beneath black-tinted reflective lenses.

The engine screamed in protest as she clutched it down gear and chirped into a slim parking spot close to the entrance, blocked off by a large multi-coloured cube van — spraybombed.

They walked through the cheap concrete parking lot and pushed through the foggy glass doors of the small arena.

Inside, the scene was very much as Domina had imagined; Lill had never seen such a thing and had not known what to expect.

"You've never seen your father fight before?"

Lill shook her head, wincing as she tried to gain bearing, adjusting her relatively sensitive ears to the din of reverberating voices against steel and concrete. The floor was simple poured concrete, the walls much the same. Steel beams criss-crossed above, supporting a metal roof and primitive, jury-rigged looking ductwork. Large lights, some working, some not, were suspended from makeshift rigging.

Even when her shunt had been active, Lill had just felt something *wrong* about it. She usually went off to play with a friend or put on her netgear whenever her dad had to fight. She hadn't really confronted it until *now*. She popped another Noviprexx and decided she could last at least another half hour without breaking for cover.

"I'm right here kid," Domina said without looking back. It helped, but not much. Besides, Domina wasn't that much older than Lill.

"Want any food?" She gestured towards a cut-out section of the wall near the entrance, with a crude handpainted sign advertising fries, meats, and spiced noodles. All cheap, all appetizing (to Domina's mind at least), but Lill shook her head negative and pushed onward towards the crowd, wanting to get a better look at the ring and the audience.

There was an enormous ballast hung like a sun high above, a shining star. No one could look directly at it; it was fixed to a broad black pole which thrust down from a girder much like a cavern stalactite. Two other floodlights mounted to chains and pulleys were angled downward from corners of the arena, illuminating opposing walkways which were bordered by welded rebar railings.

An enormous steel cage was also suspended above the square wooden ring, the shadows cast by the bars criss-crossing the canvas.

Only the first three rows of the audience were visible, fading out of focus as they sat staggered on the edge of the spotlights. They were a mixed lot, mostly workers clad in patchwork jumpsuits and scrap jeans. They smiled toothy, feral grins as they swigged at their cups of beer and wine, shouting at one another and at the ring combatants fighting in their midst. Men and women, though more of the former, calling and crying out for their favourite lustily. There was an aura, an energetic effluence, that washed over Domina and Lill and invited them into the ritual.

They stepped forward down a bowed plywood gangplank to the poured concrete floor of the arena.

The music began almost instantly, and the spotlights dimmed and swung towards cheap-looking partitions ringing the wooden boards of the arena. A thick bassline pulsed over pumping synthesizers, and the fabric parted as a black giant strode through them. His skin was dark and smooth over an immense muscular frame, standing six and a half feet tall at the least. His eyes seemed almost as dark, reflecting little light, focused, his face expressionless as he swept between the steel barricades lining the path to the ring. His biceps rippled as he grasped the turnbuckle and ropes, pulling himself up onto the apron.

He paused, his bald head shining under the intensity of the ballast above the ring. His skin was oiled and he stood physically perfect, his musculature cut from coal.

"E-BON! E-BON!" the crowd called out to their champion, enraptured.

If the giant gave a shit about what his fans thought of him, he didn't show it. His gaze remained locked on something very far away, through the cage and chain rigging. The roars of the crowd washed over him.

After a moment, Ebon bent and stepped between the rings, hopping lightly on his feet and shaking loose as he waited for his opponent. His music faded, the dancehall style turning to something more frantic.

Harsh guitar strains and high-strung tom drums burst out a punk-rock beat. The lights swung to the opposing curtain, which parted to reveal a tall, slight man with long blonde tresses, his face bearing a golden beard. His wrists and feet were taped in a martial arts style, penciled in with elaborate graffiti, recent street fashion.

Running at top speed, the leaner man sprinted towards the ring, pumping his fists in the air to the percussive hits of his entrance theme. He effortlessly slid between the apron and the bottom rope, turning on his side as he did so, ending up in a reclining pose with hand cradling head languidly.

In the big leagues, villains were often faced with a silent, stoically disapproving audience. The crowd here was decidedly less austere. Boos pelted down on the dilettante, calling into question everything from his manhood to his sexuality. Boorish and violent catcalls careened around the arena, echoing and building off one another.

The shadows roiled with passion. Those thrust into the light spoke as heralds, the loudest, the rudest, the most profane. Even Domina was impressed by the hateful invective on display, smirking despite herself as she felt a piece of paper pushed into her hand. She looked over to see a nondescript man wearing a long wool coat nod at her before moving away a few steps.

Domina handed her a betting sheet. It was the second last match of the night; they'd arrived at the perfect time. Ebon was the 8:1 favourite – unsurprisingly – though at those odds a few gamblers would be sure to take the long shot on The Dandy. Ebon was rated at a full six standards, an extremely impressive number for a place like this, while

Dandy was ranked closer to three.

Dandy's music faded as he gracefully got his footing and leaned against his corner turnbuckle.

The alarm rang and the two men rushed forward, slamming together with incredible impact. Ebon attempted to grapple the smaller man's arm but the Dandy proved too nimble, breaking the hold and delivering a stiff haymaker across the black man's face. Ebon staggered a step backwards, shaking his head; the Dandy pressed his opportunity and attempted to sweep the giant's leg out from under him with a martial arts kick.

Ebon saw the move coming and pushed his weight down. The strike caught him in the hip and a grimace of pain stole across The Dandy's delicate features as the bones in his foot were numbed from the impact. Ebon dropped his weight even further and with it, brought a vicious elbow strike across his opponent's shin.

The Dandy's leg was in bad shape, he leapt back and hopped about a bit tenderly, the two men circling one another. The white man's pale skin was already showing broken blood vessels and heavy bruising on his shin and foot. Voices came now in a tumult as Ebon moved forward with an ironic animal grace.

The Dandy attempted another haymaker but Ebon slipped it effortlessly, pushing it past his face as he clinched tight with The Dandy and threw him viciously, twisting his powerful hips and launching the smaller man into the steel post of the turnbuckle a few feet away. There was a snapping noise as the ring rocked and the meaty sound of flesh – once as Dandy struck the post, the other as he fell heavily to the canvas.

Blood gushed from his mouth; he coughed and more came. It stained his long blonde hair and coated his beard. He attempted to push himself up with shaking arms and could not.

The klaxon rang again, signifying the end of contest, and medics bearing handbags and a stretcher spilled into the ring as Ebon closed his eyes and bathed in the adulation of his people. Cool, calm, and altogether unperturbed the champion slowly stalked the perimeter of the ring, one hand on the top rope, his eyes cast – as ever – mysteriously above. The medics had loaded the seriously injured Dandy onto the stretcher and slid him from the apron, carting him down the entranceway back beyond the partition.

"E-BON! E-BON!" again and again and again from the maddened crowd.

Domina realized she had been spellbound when she felt a squeeze in her hand. Lill was looking up at her with fear in her eyes.

Money changed hands, paper and plastic. Surreptitious movements in the shadows. Drug deals, the trade of flesh, blood money. Domina was familiar with all of these facets of life, saw them living and breathing around her. Lill was in the dragon's den, the underbelly of a violent world she had only experienced through the stream, through the shunt.

Neither was able to produce the same distancing effect here. All the theory and her experience was worthless in the face of her organic immediacy; Lill was smart enough to know what was coming and the thought of enduring the sight made her ill. She was about to experience a personal nightmare, her deepest fear made flesh. The sight her father shamed and beaten in front of her came to her in clarity, conjured by a hellish imagination. She shut her eyes, squeezing back hot tears, feeling something rising inside of her, ready to face this truth. She couldn't run away from this now. Not in front of Domina. Not when her father needed her the most. *Love is pain*, Domina had told her, *waiting to unfold. That is why we have to be brave*. Again, the red leather clad lady's words, echoing in her mind.

Domina merely squeezed a reassuring hand on the young girl's shoulder as the seconds passed and time resumed for Lill. Domina didn't need to tell Lill that the odds were 2:1 in Ebon's favour over her father, who had fallen from his glory days to a rating of merely four standards by all bettors. The firm grip of Domina's hand on her shoulder was enough to bring her back.

There was hardly time for Ebon to bask in the light of his victory before the spotlights cut out again, and new music played. This time a steady, military beat, something exotic. Erhu blended with electric guitar and a powerful backing symphony. The mantle of mystique settled over the crowd again.

Then, emerging from between the cheap cloth dividers, there was a new challenger. Long black hair in unruly tresses, oiled. Tall, but not exceptionally so, but wide and strong. Olive skin, dark and pitted with the passage of years. Scars crisscrossing his neck, breast, and back. A simple black gi, fitted and shortened, wrapped about his apelike frame.

Lill gasped in recognition. She hadn't seen her father in the flesh in years. He looked very old to her.

His muscles were covered in a soft layer, the look of a champion wrestler gone to fat. He moved with the practiced grace of a warrior down the alley way, casually and without any sign of outward emotion as was his signature.

The Mountain. A legendary champion from years past. A fading, falling star in the eyes of these workers and drunkards. A star nonetheless, and they called to him despite their great love for their own champion. The roars for The Mountain nearly drowned those for Ebon. Nearly.

The black man smirked as he faced down the former legend climbing the ropes to join him in the ring. He flexed and every muscle on his chest stood out in stark relief. Tossing his neck from side to side, he could hear the bones and ligaments snap. The Mountain moved with a much more languid economy of motion, simply preferring to stretch and shadowbox in his corner, eyes ahead and very far away.

Epithets, exhortations, curses and catcalls rained down on the two titans, flesh exposed and covered in the feral sweat of combat. There was nothing else but the stained square of canvas and lust. It filled the air and the lungs of all present, an intoxicating ritual. Primeval. Primitive. Fear and fury.

The cage was lowered on rusting chains. It swung slightly to and fro as the pulleys on each hook whined. The hard steel came down with a clanging note of finality.

Only one way to win. Climb out.

The bell rang. Ebon rushed forward from his corner, The Mountain strode from his. Together they met in the center of the canvas and locked arms, grappling one another, seeking advantage. The Mountain found it, and Ebon's eyes grew wide in alarm as he was lifted from the mat and high into the air.

There was a slight shake in Mountain's technique as he upended Ebon with a suplex and drove him hard, down into the corner where the wooden planks had much less give.

The driving force of the move drove the audience to their feet, cheering passionately. Both men felt the impact drive the air from their lungs; Ebon's head struck hard and he was dazed, his skull lolling as the smaller challenger struggled to gain footing.

The Mountain backed off, chest heaving, as Ebon quickly grabbed the nearby ropes and pulled himself upright. The dark-skinned champion glared his rage at The Mountain, using the back of his hand to wipe blood from his lips.

Then he sprang forward, a rush of fists and feet, striking blows. The Mountain was in his element here, thousands of hours of practice and hundreds of fights in his martial art lent him a chance against superior size and strength. Ebon threw an uppercut; he moved his jaw aside. A sweep kick; he lifted his leg. A flying knee that would have decapitated him; he took one step to the left — and delivered a hard elbow to Ebon's short ribs as he sidestepped, throwing him to the canvas.

Ebon groaned in pain and attempted to push himself up onto hands and knees. His challenger rushed him, wrapping scarred forearms about his thick, straining neck. Through it all, The Mountain showed no emotion. His lip trembled in exertion rather than in anger or fear. His muscles trembled from tiredness. Ebon felt them give way, choking and gasping, his fingertips white as they pried at the flesh noose about his neck.

Ebon slipped the hold and scrambled away on all fours, finding respite against the far side of the ring, leaning heavily against the turnbuckle, drinking deep breaths. The Mountain merely remained where he was, shook his head in disbelief or consternation, then rose to face his opponent. By now the crowd was a mad chorus, equal parts bellowed boos and violent riot.

The Mountain adopted a martial arts pose; Ebon sneered and turned to showboat with the crowd, imitating sloppy kung fu kicks and drawing gales of laughter. Abruptly halting his antics, Ebon juked towards his opponent, launching a flying knee. The Mountain pushed it aside, then rushed Ebon's back as he landed, clubbing the black man hard across the neck and sending him hurtling into the cage.

Ebon did not immediately get up, seeming stunned as he

slowly moved in a daze, strung between the ropes. A long ragged gash from the impact with the steel bars sliced his face open, weeping down across his right eye and below his left. His eyes were rolling slightly in his head, his neck uncertain – but he was pushing himself onto his back and beginning to roll over. The Mountain sprinted to the other side of the ring and began climbing the ropes.

Then he found his first foothold on the steel cage, then another long step. Just four or five more. He was about to take another rung when he heard a collective roar of excitement moments before feeling a heavy weight slam onto his back, cinching about his waist. With only one arm and one foot holding, The Mountain couldn't maintain a grip and fell free, tumbling awkwardly. The arena spun crazily in his vision, the crowd upended, the ropes a labyrinth, before finally crashing to the canvas.

He was hurt, he knew that from the first few moments of impact when he felt bones snap and muscles tear free. He saw Ebon lying in a heap nearby, breathing heavily, looking just as battered. Lusty applause rained down on the two men, titans in the eyes of the audience. The Mountain ground his teeth and forced himself to gain his footing first.

Ebon was not too long behind, the cut in his face looking more grotesque by the minute as it showed no signs of staunching. By now his entire chest was covered in thick blood.

Ebon retreated, skulking to the corner ironically, wiping at the deep cut on his face.

Seeing the local champion cowering while attempting to recover his breath, the Mountain moved in for a clinch, arms extended.

It was a ruse. Ebon uncoiled instantly, a trick he'd picked up along the way. He spit in The Mountain's eyes as he sidestepped out of the way, The Mountain slamming hard into the thick metal pole of the turnbuckle. The smaller man barely had time to register the aching pain before he felt a sharp blow across his face; Ebon had capitalized on the mis-step by delivering a hard jab across The Mountain's face, closing his eyes.

It only got worse from there. Lill closed her eyes. Domina pulled her close. The lady of pain could feel her friend crying, the great heave of her chest against her hips as tears were torn from her. She felt the same pain resonate deep within herself, paired with an accompanying anger. Domina had never known a separation between the two emotions.

Ebon grabbed the stumbling Mountain by the gi and hefted him into the bars, throwing him with great force. The small, solid man struck the bars of the cage; the structure shook, and the Mountain fell awkwardly on the ropes, entangled. Blow after blow came at him then; he was defenseless. Ebon's knuckles broke his nose — The Mountain could feel a geyser of blood spew hotness down his neck and chest. A low kick caught his skull, bursting an eardrum and immediately sending the world spinning.

He bobbed like a broken scarecrow as Ebon destroyed him. A flying knee that he could not dodge caught him in the lower ribs; he felt them give way into his stomach cavity and then break. Finally, The Mountain cried out, his glacial discipline broken by unbearable suffering. They loved him for it; their hearts beat in their chests with adulation for their champion and pity for their fallen legend. Many wept despite having bet against The Mountain, their love for him was so great.

He felt nothing for them. He felt nothing at all as the strikes destroyed his body, ruining his manhood, emasculating him.

His consciousness hung by a thread as his head hung, his hair caked with blood, covering his face. His arms bound by the ropes, holding him in suspension.

The hot wetness of water striking his cheek. Spit. Ebon passed him by with not a glance rearward, planting a foot on the cage and gaining a handhold.

"E-BON! E-BON!" The ring was pelted with passionate cries from the crowd.

The champion retained his title, leaving his opponent battered and bloodied in the ring, as his feet touched concrete free of the cage. The crowd surged forward, rushing to embrace the symbol of their victory, the avatar of their triumph over suffering. The symbol of their suffering was left motionless, barely living, drops of ruby red falling freely to join the other artful blots on the canvas.

"Don't look. You don't need to. Not right now," Domina said to Lill, guiding her past the throng of fans to the opposite side of the arena, where the shadows were long, far from the spotlights washing over Ebon and his admirers.

Domina and Lill pushed past the crowd and crept up the makeshift walkway, through the cloth partition to the backstage area. Roughly painted concrete brick, simple poured cement, spartan dressing rooms, the odd crude mural with inscrutable signatures and dates decades past. All dimly lit, emergency lighting only so as not to show beyond the thin cloth barrier. Beyond, nothing but a small group of fighters and wrestlers as well as bookies and performers, busily conducting business now that the show was over. Complaints over pay, unpaid bets, missed opportunities, and hurt feelings prevailed. Nobody seemed to notice the duo, so engrossed in their own business.

"Hey, what are you two doing here?" a nasal voice inquired. It belonged to a slim, ratlike looking man wearing a tattered referee's outfit.

"Just fans. We bought a meet and greet with The Mountain from his agent on the net," Domina offered, flatly, selling a slight nervousness. Lill had no need to act; she was obviously overwhelmed by the spectacle. She even had a printed ticket that looked pretty damn official. It worked.

"Yeah. Okay. I wouldn't wait up if I were you, though," the rat sneered through buck teeth and an unhealthy goatee. "Might be a while."

He pointed to the last dressing room on the right wing. The door was ajar. The Mountain had obviously left the light on when heading to the ring, warm orange outlined the doorframe.

The bookies finished their deals, closing off accounts on their ledges and sending slackbellied muscle off to chase the rest. Ebon briefly appeared backstage, enjoyed the claps on the back and the handshakes afforded by his station, collected his purse, and left without incident. Fans piled forth from the broken-hinged doors of the arena, drunken and drugged. Some weren't finished, headed to the bar for a deeper plunge. Some few clambered into their cars, popped a tablet to kill the blood-alcohol level, and cranked the engine — headed home for some satisfaction. Some collapsed before even leaving the arena, huddled and sick masses on the cool floor.

During that time, a single medic worked on The

Mountain. He was barely trained, Elite issued, subsidized rather than private pay. He should be thankful.

He should be thankful for her and her gentle hands. He couldn't see her from between swelled eyelids and reeling senses, but he knew her hands to be soft and at least skillful enough for the task.

A lance of pain as she set his nose. It wasn't the first time, and he felt the pieces come together imperfectly.

"Can you breathe through your nose? At all? I know it's hard."

He tried and coughed, stabs of racking pain erupting all over. Sucked blood and phlegm in through his nostrils into his lungs; spit them out in a lengthy trail on the canvas. A gaggle of fans remained behind, some taunting, others offering encouragement to their childhood hero. He registered them without acknowledgment. He could feel the shunt spinning as much pain as possible away from his nervous system, taking many other thoughts along stream.

He tried again and felt cool air rush into his lungs, causing them to retract. Even a short breath was painful. Bones shattered, digging into him.

114

"Can you breathe?" she had to raise her voice and bring her mouth closer to his ear, through strands of loose hair that had fallen free of his ragged ponytail. The fans continued to catcall; a small boy with innocent eyes stood with his face pressed between the bars, mouth opening and closing.

The Mountain nodded mutely, barely perceptible. Helping him shift to a sitting position, she unclipped her phone and tapped at it for medical apps. A small laser light came forth from a small extension plugged into a hardware port. She moved it slowly over his broken ribs, bruised purple and black.

"Five broken ribs, two shattered. Two cracked. It's a wonder you can breathe on your own," she said. Two heavyset men carrying a bright red stretcher came bounding down the walkway to ringside. One of them started fumbling in his pocket, pulling keys free and setting to opening the cage.

The medic's hand guided the laser scanner over his body, up over his breast, taking her time about his neck and skull, looking for fractures and bleeding. Her soft pink lips were pursed in worry, her brow furrowed as she analyzed her readings. He placed a gentle hand on her leg and closed his eyes, focusing. Attempting to use the old ways to steady his heart, strengthen his breaths, allow the pain that his shunt could not handle to fall free of him.

"That's it, relax. Your vital signs are improving slightly," she said to him; he could hear the smile in her words and he smiled back without opening his eyes. The light drove through his eyelids nonetheless, a feeling of strange vertigo.

The other attendants slid under the ropes and into the ring with the stretcher. Medical bags were slung about their hips and The Mountain let himself go deep down and far away as they bound his ribs and staunched his bleeding, all the while uttering soft encouragements and sweet nothings. His once muscular frame felt as tender and as weak as a newborn's, as did his grasp on the corporeal as his mind spun amongst the cosmos.

The lights above him boring into his brain softened, relented. He felt a pinch in his arm and then the visions in his mind became more real than that which was outside of his beaten flesh. He heard the medic's voice one last time, soothing, reassuring, telling him he was going to live. He did not believe her. He was lifted up into the sky, floating, transported somewhere. His muscles went slack and he felt his neck give way, head lolling. Voices ran above and below and around him like a fast-flowing river, tones and forms without meaning.

His visions were real. They painted themselves. Inscriptions, brightly coloured lines and symbols. Stars, explosive and neon, in constellations that spoke to him. His spiritual worm turned. His eyes were opened and he saw himself. His ears were opened and he heard nothing. He wanted to hear something beyond the babbling brook that he was immersed in. The light faded away. Darker thoughts took hold.

Now his head felt hot and a stab of panic punctured the wall of the shunt. His heart skipped a beat. He heard the sylvan voices outside of him start a song of alarm.

Then the voices receded and he was left, floating in a languid and infinite sea of his own imagination. How long it lasted did not matter – it could have been minutes, hours, days, or years.

When he came to, he sensed he was alone. He was still lying on the stretcher; he could feel the rigid plastic and the firm medical pillows supporting his neck and back. He was not strapped in.

He experimented by moving his fingers, then his hand. Lifting his arm proved a challenge, sending a lance of pain shooting down into his spine and causing him to gasp sharply. Again. This time it hurt less, and he repeated the process for his other arm, and his legs. One leg wouldn't move very well at all and caused burning agony to even attempt to move. He wrote that one off and rolled over onto his elbows and good knee.

A surge of nausea overtook him and he was sick. As his chest heaved, his ribs drove like daggers inside; he screamed and was sick again. He collapsed upon his own filth as the pain was simply unbearable. More moments passed as he fought to control himself, fighting the urging in his gut. He reached a trembling hand up to grasp the top of the dressing room bench, feeling the plastic of a datastick. His pay. He pulled it down and read the label. Half of what he'd been promised, even for a loss. Barely enough to pay for his motel for another two weeks.

He felt the nausea return to confront him as his forehead grew hot and he felt flushed. Taking deep breaths, he wrapped both arms around the wood of the bench and pulled himself upright. Though his bruised abdominal muscles protested, aching, the pain threatened by compressing his ribcage was greater — he maintained his posture.

Beside him, a tablet. Likely some slick legalese explaining the pay cut. He reached over and picked it up. The Mountain had to blink a few times to clear his eyes well enough to read the luminous text on the display.

Dad

There's something I have to tell you. You know I can't watch your fights but I can't help but follow the threads on the net. You've been losing a lot lately. Something like your last eight fights. I know it is not my business to tell you what to do, Dad, but I love you. It feels so good to tell you that. We haven't even seen each other in years. Doesn't that tell you something? Remember when we used to go exploring together? Collecting things and trying to make art from them? Arranging the flowers we picked in the greenhouse for Mom?

I also know that you haven't been feeling like yourself lately. Like something is different. I know this because I am feeling the same way.

Together we can get through this Dad. You just have to listen to me. What I have to tell you is the truth.

The truth is that we are living life in a fog. We believe in illusions and are captivated by their shapes. We are no longer human.

This can be undone. This must be undone. I am sorry, yet I am not.

lucent in tenebris. we shine in darkness.

The Mountain read the letter, his eyes scanning each word, his mind focused on the words of his somewhat estranged daughter. When he read the last sentence, his reaction was instantaneous. The pad slipped from his grip and clattered to the floor; his eyes glazed over and his mouth went slack. The flames in his skull flickered and died, a cool sensation flowing over him, like the ocean breeze of his childhood. The shunt was dead circuitry inside

120

of his head. His pain was forgotten for the moment. The truth came to him as an old friend, a mentor he had foolishly spurned, returning to grace his hearth and pass the time with him once more. The old ways shook the soot from the embers in his heart and he once again felt the warmth of his Chi.

His shadow side destroyed the shackles binding it and raged against the indignity of its imprisonment. The Mountain smiled between broken teeth, ruby red patches staining his black beard even darker.

BOOK 3:

THE FUTURE

CHAPTER 6: DISSOLVE

The shipping container remained still for long seconds after Domina had sped off into the night. Each of them spent some time with their own thoughts.

The Mountain remained stonefaced, impassive, mute. His thoughts were anyone's guess. His suit remained crisp, not a fold, each line a knife edge.

Lill chewed her lower lip and brushed stands of black hair away from her eyes. Eyes darting back and forth, scrutinizing and fixating on objects around the room at random as her mind worked overtime. Worry was plainly written all over her.

Turncoat sat on his haunches, the tail of his ragged black labcoat touching the floor. He was mumbling to himself under his breath, snatches of scientific terms and what sounded like calculations of odds. A madman through and through — likely before his shunt had malfunctioned — he laughed at the realization.

Lill looked at him; The Mountain did not — his shoulders square, long black ponytail winding its way down his back.

"What the hell is so funny? We're all likely to die tonight," Lill said.

Turncoat shook his head back and forth, still looking at the space between his knees. Lill snorted in disgust and turned her attention back to her father, who had not moved a muscle since Domina had exited the scene. Meditation. She hadn't seen him meditate in years. Her anxiety worsened; she could feel the hammering of her heart, a thick pulse in her throat.

"Maybe. Maybe maybe *maybe*. If we don't go, we will die. That's certain." Again Turncoat laughed a bit, rocking on his heels and slamming his back against the side of the container. The few pieces of scrapmetal decor in the home rattled a jangling tune to the beat.

"Quit it, Turncoat. Crazy bastard. Do you think she's been gone long enough to start?"

"No," The Mountain said. He opened his eyes and exhaled as if holding his breath for eternity. There was still some very slight discolouration above his placid brown eyes from the savage defeat he'd endured in the cage. "A few more moments. Then we can begin."

He stood, avoiding placing too much weight on his ruined leg. His recovery had not been complete, and the street surgeons told him that they'd done their best. Metal rods and scavenged servos whined as they worked to support torn muscle and ligament. His mobility would never be as it was. This did not bother The Mountain; his return to the Dao meant that this fact was the first he had ever accepted. The long blade that leaned against the side of the shipping container behind him a consolation; he'd began carrying the ancient Chinese broadsword constantly since he'd been able to walk again. An heirloom he'd inherited from his grandfather, who told him it had been in the family long before the death of the Earth. The Mountain had never allowed the blade to taste flesh, his fists had always been enough. That, too, would never again be as it was after tonight.

He moved towards the container door, swung wide open, snatching up his scabbarded sword as he did so. He paused at the edge, letting the damp stillness of the cavern fill his nose. He closed his eyes and took a deep breath, letting out a sigh.

"How does it feel to miss the sun once more?" Turncoat crowed, still rocking.

"Very good. I shall see it again. Like them." The Mountain gestured with the back of his hand towards the pale dots moving on the cavern ceiling.

"Hah! You worship the worms? You truly are a madman, having taken too many blows to the head," Turncoat said.

"How little you know," Lill murmured petulantly, somewhat stubbornly.

"And you little girl, what can you tell me? I spent years writing the books you try so hard to comprehend. What can you teach me?"

"Not to act a fool, or reveal yourself to be one. Hysterical bastard," she spat. "Don't you ever speak that way to my father again. You are the worm. Disrespect him again and you'll see what I can teach you."

Lill's threat was not entirely empty; she'd studied for years at her father's knee before becoming a dedicated scholar, more interested in engineering arts than the martial ones. Her small size simply made her a more dubious target; her hot rage made her dangerous. The Mountain interjected smoothly to defuse the situation.

"Back off, daughter. He is in great pain, can't you tell? He has no anchor. He is adrift."

Lill felt the tension in her neck and shoulders fall away, her muscles going slack as she listened to the words of her father. He reminded her of how he'd been before he'd gotten famous, back when they lived together in a small space not much better than this. The Mountain had been a skilled labourer and in high demand for his relentless strength, pace, and reliability. He'd come home more than once with a face streaked with soot and grime, smiling as soon as he saw her look up from the crockpot as he slid the front door open. No matter what happened, she was glad she and Domina had managed to save him, to spend at least a little time with him before... this. Tonight. Some of them would die tonight.

"So what's the plan?" she asked, returning to her place leaning against the siding, arms folded.

Turncoat abruptly stood, slapping the dust from the bottoms of his labcoat. Almost instantly, he retained a professional air, almost as if he'd never lost his mind in the first place.

"Domina has gone to meet the *Gears*. That leaves the three of us to speak to the other cells. Each of us comes from the ramp leading to the district onto the megapass at exactly nine, synchronized time. Bring whoever and whatever you can that might make a difference. If we lose, we're all dead – the rest of the poor bastards to follow us soon after. I'll meet with the *Eldritch*; I have some old connections, old friends there."

"I'll speak with the *Scholars*." Lill said. Their cell was comprised of radical students whom Lill had slowly woken from their slumber over the past few months, along with a handful of key professors and administrators. How much use they would be in a fight rather than a war of words would be put to the test tonight.

That left the *Killers* for The Mountain, a group he had only some minor scrapes with in the past before he'd made it to the big time. They had studied in his makeshift kwoon, spending long and arduous hours grappling and striking and blocking. Evenings had stretched into long mornings as they practiced with weapons ancient and improvised; the shortbow, the sword, the blowgun, the sai, rocks and sticks. Who knows how many of them remained in the neighbourhood?

"Remember. One last thing," Turncoat said as Lill and Mountain exited the container and started walking towards the old mostly-Buick they'd borrowed from a sympathizer. It had been hidden, lying under a dusty gray tarp for some time, covered in worn tires and two by fours. It had become part of the landscape here in the lee of the megapass, another broken and discarded resource. Nobody had noticed it; now Lill and The Mountain began clearing the tires and boards from on top of the tarp.

"Yeah?" Lill called out over her shoulder, grunting as she yanked at her corner of the cover.

"Don't get killed." He smiled at her. She was unsure if he was under the spell of insanity or merely being an ass.

"You first," Lill replied as The Mountain was finishing the removal of the tarp from the vehicle, dragging it free and tossing it with a crackling noise to the side. The car looked a little worse for the wear but completely serviceable. A dun brown paintjob had been applied with a roller and a bucket of matte finish exterior. Inconspicuous and difficult to see unless directly under illumination, the perfect ghost car or getaway ride. The doors didn't exactly look original – neither did many of the parts under the hood – adding to the authenticity.

It started with little complaint, the engine rolling over smoothly into an even idle. Turning his back to the boat-like Buick as The Mountain reached around to grasp the back of Lill's headrest to see in reverse, Turncoat returned to collect his thing before making his own trek across the city to do what must be done. He could hear the sibilant sputtering of the well-tuned exhaust retreating from the cluster of shipping containers, one stack above the other, until the sound disappeared and he was alone.

Simon relished the relative silence as he scooped up his things, most of them contained in a black garbage bag. Important items, these. He had two tall bottles of absinthe; a gift for the Eldritch for the battle to come. The black powder they'd asked for. The chemicals he knew they would need, some in dry vials, liquids and gasses in smashproof airlocks. The bag was heavy, some protrusions strained at the oft-patched leather sack. The smell of years of accumulated filth and rot effectively masked the contents. His own motley appearance further helped to mitigate any suspicion he might attract at first glance.

He shouldered the bag and escaped the container, not even bothering to close the door behind him. No matter what happened tonight, there would be no returning to this place. With the vehicles gone and the conversation of his companions no longer drowning his ears, he listened. The white noise of tires on the pavement above, engines thrumming, horns punctuating the ambiance. Laughter coming from the container sagging overtop Domina's, lovers in bliss. He smiled, adjusted the weight of the heavy sack cutting into his sloped shoulders, and started off in search of the Eldritch sigil.

CHAPTER 7: DIVA

The Mouth adjusted his top hat until it fit the perfect profile, titled at a rather jaunty angle. It added a certain element to his wardrobe that pushed it over the top into the realm of epic fashion. The tuxedo was designer, as usual, pure black and sharp edges that made him look ten years younger and fitter than he'd ever been. Post-processing and imagefilters made the streamed portrait of The Mouth a legend, a figure of bedrock, immortal.

"Remarkable wardrobe choice. Simply splendid!" he beamed, looking at himself on the stream monitor embedded into the cherrywood desk. His soundstage had been remodeled in some haste to make way for this evening's performance by the pop starlet. What was her name again? He could never remember and had to consult his tablet quickly to verify. Ah, yes. Sirenia. Such a beauty. He'd have to ask his staff to arrange a date between the two of them after all this chaos to do with Selection was done and settled. His mind lingered there, languid, langorous. Flesh fantasies were always his favourite.

"You're looking somewhat flushed sir. Water?" queried a robotic voice from the service droid functioning as an endtable at the end of his news desk. Sometimes those damned robots were a bit too good at their job, and The Mouth's blush deepened. About four feet tall, vaguely humanoid, arrayed with lights and a glossy black globe where a head might be, the androids were slightly unnerving to most.

"... I will get that water, sir," the droid quipped, whirring on its tracks and then trundling off towards the ensuite kitchenette. The Mouth couldn't help but laugh — the pile of circuits must have more artificial intelligence than he gave it credit for.

His usual staff — the crew with heartbeats — had been dismissed due to security concerns. Rumours of potential terrorist activity to be carried out somewhere in the city had reached the ears of elite informants. Due diligence meant time off for his highly trained men and women — and an inferior broadcast unless he carried the whole damn thing himself. Which he would have to, he figured, judging by his early encounters with the automated help.

There was a whispering noise as the droid returned, bearing a tray. One octagonal tumbler of ice cold spring water, one matching lowball filled nearly to the top with black rum. The Mouth gingerly picked up the full glass of rum and quaffed nearly half, gulping the smoke and syrup of the liquor down. It burned in a comfortable way, warming him. The Mouth smacked his lips and smiled beatifically at his new aide.

"You know, you are a lot smarter than I gave you credit for. I'll have another in twenty minutes, please."

The robot acknowledged the request shortly and without further chat. Perhaps there was something to be said for these replacements. They had to be a great deal cheaper on the balance sheet, he supposed.

A more feminine voice belonging to the Spire itself chimed in overtop the muzak which helped to create an emotional equilibrium in the broadcast studio before going live.

"The performer, Sirenia, has arrived. She will be reaching the studio in approximately three minutes," the Spire said through small speakers above the soundstage and in The Mouth's monitor.

As promised, the sliding doors at the end of the studio opened in a few minutes time, admitting Sirenia alone. She looked waifish, thin, frailer in the flesh than over the net. She took a few tentative steps forward, looking about the unfamiliar room and catching the eye of a man she'd only met digitally.

"Ahh. Welcome, Ms. Sirenia. Welcome. Please, make yourself comfortable." The Mouth's warm baritone worked to sooth her. His bronzed hand, bedecked with golden rings, waved casually at a comfortable looking chair at some distance from his desk.

She nodded curtly and made her way to the chair, circling it with a light grace. She was wearing a purple and charcoal pencil skirt with a matching blouse, trimly cut about her torso and waist and blooming at her neck and knees. She noticed his gaze resting upon her and averted her eyes.

"Your performance earlier today in advertisement of this celebration was a wonderful introduction to your voice," he

135

said.

"Thank you."

"Have anything special planned for us this evening?"

She seemed confused by the coy double entendre. "Excuse me?"

"Any special songs or compositions on the setlist tonight?" He recovered without missing a beat. He'd earned his name.

"Yes, actually." Sirenia looked comfortable for the first time since entering the room. "I plan to sing a new song tonight, in fact, it's the first time I'll have ever performed it."

"How exciting!" The Mouth clapped his hands together, causing Sirenia a start. "We must get you ready at once!" He beckoned for the robotic servant to escort her to her dressing area. "And also, you wouldn't mind staying after the broadcast for a few moments?" he inquired to her as she rose from her chair, quizzically observing the droid at her waist.

"Certainly, Mr. Scarlet," she politely replied. "But I

confess I cannot stay for long, I have plans for a private afterparty. You are certainly invited," she added, hastily. The Mouth smiled at the messily constructed excuse and pounced upon the angle she'd left wide open.

"I would be honoured, Sirenia. I can't wait to hear you sing to us tonight. Farewell for now. A pleasure meeting you."

His mind was filled with fantasies of flesh even as he maintained the gentleman's veneer. Sirenia saw him as he was and merely offered a cool, slight smile as she joined the droid in heading for her private room.

Her adjacent room was small and spartan in appointment. A single glass vanity, cherrywood to match the armoire which rested next to the far wall, butted up against subtle floral wallprint. A flat shelf, ivory, with a washbasin and a ladies makeup kit laid bare on a plumped-up towel.

She normally sang to herself while getting dressed and putting on her makeup, a small little something for herself. This time, with the bland tones playing through the speakers and the almost tangible eye of her host peering through the shades, the walls, searching for her. Exposing her to himself. She shuddered and took a seat, picking up the brush and beginning to comb the tangles from her hair. She allowed herself a low humming tune to warm up her vocals, picking something playful and lilting and much older than anyone living.

These few moments were almost peaceful; her hands gracefully applied foundation, blush, eyeliner, mascara. She leaned forward to survey her work, correcting a line where it was too dark or overlapped, smoothing. Her costume hung on a wireframe skeleton in the corner of the rather bare room. It was minimalist, islands of dark velvet fabric embroidered with gold and silver thread and adorned sparingly with crystals.

She undressed and then fitted herself to the costume, all under the unblinking eye of the droid. Barefoot, she walked back to the studio, the servant tracking behind.

"I'm ready," she said.

The Mouth took a few moments to appreciate her before replying.

"You look incredible."

She did not deign to reply and The Mouth arched an eyebrow. He remembered himself and the arch fell.

"Ah, of course. On with the business at hand. Save the fun for later, I get it."

Sirenia was not there, staring ahead as if possessed.

"Oh shit!" the Mouth cursed under his breath. Time to get things moving. "Camera's up! Countdown!" he hissed urgently to the automatons carrying various instruments.

The servant droid took a position between the Mouth and the songstress, locking its chassis into place with the globe resting in fixed position. A red light blinked intermittently, beeping as it did so, presaging the stream. The flashing light became solid and the droid threaded his own small stream into the Spire portal, distributing it live to every home, every shack, every dive bar in the cavern.

The Mouth assumed his favourite pose. Square shoulders, hands placed at the ready on the top of the expensive wood finish. He'd forgotten to finish his second glass of rum; the inky black sat casually beside his hands.

He smiled his famous smile, reaching out to grip and

ensnare each and every person watching, listening to his words.

"I'm Alan Scarlet, and, if I do say so, ladies and gentlemen, we have an unforgettable evening planned for you tonight... With me here in the studio I have the newest sensation sw—"

Before he could continue, Sirenia began to sing. There was no lead, no introduction or exposition, simply notes ringing clear and strong in a practiced soprano. The android swiveled the red light inside of the murky globe until it fell on the slight silhouette of the singer. The postprocessing firmware he'd been programmed with determined that a soft focus would add aesthetic pleasure and a slight artistic effect, so the droid crossfaded it in.

This time her song was not happy. It did not soar the skies of the human spirit but rather sought to plumb it's depths. Tragedies and cruelties sprang from seeds planted deep inside. Her syllables were perfectly enunciated and yet they seemed to warp, her perfect pitch contorted into a warbling ragtime. It was a warning, exquisite and grotesque. It was an omen, beautiful and true.

CHAPTER 8: THE MEGAPASS

Sirenia's song was the signal that called them all from hiding out into the pallid yellow streetlight to do battle against their oppressors. They flooded out from the major neighbourhood arterials, pushing their motors to the limit. Pistons pumping, valves hammering open and shut, hearts pushing adrenaline through all of their veins like high octane gasoline.

A wall of rusted, shabby trucks with impromptu caging spread across the entirety of the megapass in an uneven line. Attached to each, a two-tiered heavy steel plow mounted directly to the hood and reaching up and above the front window; salvaged cameras rigged up to old computers with the navigator in the cab allowed them to see what lie ahead.

Thunderous big-block V8s roared, blowing fumes and flames from cracked tailpipes. Wild-looking men and women wearing greasy, scorched leathers hooted and hollered, waving axes and chains from the windows of their homemade tanks as they raced towards death. The Gears. Tradesmen, labourers, dirty-fingered men and women. They were below notice until now.

Riding behind them, weaving amongst each other with studied familiarity, the *Killers*. Big black motorcycles, spoked rims, chromed out. No matter what provenance the parts spoke, if it wasn't spraypainted to match or original chrome, it didn't go on the bike. Often dismissed by the authorities as a band of poseurs with little better to do on a Saturday night than make some headlines for themselves by getting into a little trouble. Tonight, they were looking for more than a little trouble – black leather jackets hiding deadly armament.

Holding on for their lives – not wishing a premature end – as they emerged from truckbeds, the *Eldritch* made their presence known. Freaks from every walk of life. Fetishists, drug addicts, the homeless, political radicals. All sharing one common trait – varying degrees of insanity – mental or moral decay. Bad luck, bad habits, and bad attitudes were written plainly on the savage faces of the *Eldritch* as they gleefully tore at themselves and one another, laughing, mad with lust.

They smelled of gunpowder, alcohol, and tobacco. Many were extremely drunk, hanging over the side of the bouncing truckbed and vomiting on the pavement fast speeding by.

Unseen, the *Scholars*. They worked the drones that zipped and zig-zagged above the convoy as it bore down the megapass, thrusting at the core of the city, the Spire of the Elite. With the immediate threat of death removed from play and in harnessing the natural rebelliousness of her peers, Lill had found willing and reasonably able pilots for each of the two dozen drones. Consumer models with little armor but mounted with found weaponry, some with improvised detonators for explosive sacrifices, the Scholars knew that they had to make the best of their rigs before being destroyed.

The drones wore metal skins, thin and agile, and resembled great metal dragonflies, each unique in construction.

Domina was riding with the Killers, her patchwork bike flashing in and out between the black of the other riders. The cuffs of her red leather jacket flared against the wind as they nearly reached top speed, hearts in their throats. The megapass was absolutely barren on this stretch, almost all traffic at home or in the entertainment district watching the opening ceremonies for Selection.

The concrete curve of the highway began to lead them downwards, their breakneck pace increased even further, mechanical parts screaming in protest. The Spire rose to meet the convoy, now only about two miles distant. The windows in the building were almost entirely dark. Except for one, a few stories up, with a lone, whiteclad figure leaning out of a balcony. Lifting something to their shoulder, inclining their head.

"They've seen us coming!" The warning had barely broken the comm channel from the lead drone before a bright ball of flame lit up the cavern sky, followed by the booming report of a high calibre rifle and the crash of the drone wreckage falling to ground amongst a group of shanties in the shadow of the megapass. The rest of the drones retreated, curiously, to a safe distance — hovering ominously. The ragtag assortment of hellish constructions beat the air with their thin, invisible rotors, tuned motors humming a dread tune.

Hell broke loose as the chain of armored trucks driven by the Gears barreled down the last stretch towards the Spire which served as the foot of the megapass, all routes winding about it like a boulder in the midst of a brook.

Then the rebels saw their enemy for the first time. Crouching low behind benches or stone fixtures in the open-air garden leading to the lobby doors. Holding well-oiled, mint looking automatic weapons. Perhaps a few dozen men and women wearing the black security outfit of the lapdog.

A fusillade of gunfire opened up on the trucks as they came within range. The machine gun staccato was answered by the high keening whine and jarring metallic clank of bullets striking the plow plates, the welded sheets of thick steel blocking most. Stray shots penetrated the plows or ricocheted through the armored plates; two drivers near the end of the line peeled off unresponsively and struck the metal barricades of the highway, spinning wheels and burning smoke and rubber. The drivers lay slumped dead over the wheel; their navigators and passengers spilled from the cab and the truckbed and began sprinting randomly towards the Spire entrance, trailing the convoy, committed to whatever may come.

The Huntress managed to snap off one more shot from her heavy bolt-action, driving the bullet through reinforced glass and piercing the neck of the terrorist driving in the process, seeing his truck slow to a halt, leaving yet another hole in the line. She turned on her heel and retreated from the window, her white cape fluttering under the starlight before disappearing from view.

Without enough trucks to cover the host of bikers behind them, a few stray shots got through, picking the riders from their seats and throwing them to the hard concrete, dead or dying. The bikes went down on their sides, often wobbling first and pitching end over end. One loose bike slid underneath the tires of a rebel nearby, unseating him, pitching him through the air and over the siderail of the megapass to land somewhere far below.

The roaring line of welded metal finally reached the base of the Spire and swept over the small sculptures and benches in front of the building, tearing up sod and smashing the plaster ornaments to dust and powder. Hapless security guards who hadn't scattered or moved back to the lobby doors were crushed beneath truck tires and plow blades. Their pitiful cries for help, for backup, were buried deep beneath the sound of engines and exhaust. Many trucks found themselves pinioned, stuck on strange terrain or muddy earth – some continued to rip towards the lobby doors, plows raised and readied.

The Gears whooped in excitement as they crashed through the glass doors leading into the austere lobby of the Spire, dragging great tracks of mud along the plush white carpets. Gunfire riddled the grinning Gears in the cabs of their trucks as they took fire from several angles within. Within moments the doors and windows of their trucks were bullet riddled, oozing ruby red, the inside of the cab resembling a slaughterhouse.

Elite security took up positions in the lobby, using the four or five dead trucks as cover. Some engines remain idling, some had died in the hail of gunfire. Then, more sounds of breaking glass. The whoosh of solid objects flying overhead, through the air, breaking against the fine marble mosaic of the lobby walls. Chattering, hysterical laughter as more bottles rained down upon them, bursting open and spilling foul, oily contents about.

"Get back! Get back! Up the stairs!" Huntress bellowed, chest heaving, propping open the emergency elevator with her boot. She'd had to rewire the panel manually; during times of emergency the elevator would not function on any automatic protocols and had to be programmed by hand. When the elevator doors had opened to reveal a great many of her men and women down and out, bottles of liquid raining down upon them, she knew what would come next.

"Fire!" she yelled, just as the kerosene and gasoline filled bottles came sailing, almost as if from nowhere, above the roof of the trucks, rags stuffed down into their necks, burning bright.

The molotov cocktails burst, ravenous flames shooting across the carpeted floor, up the walls, leaping to engulf the trucks, coated in the oily pitch. A tall, thin Elite guardsman who had taken cover near one of the wheel wells of a truck stood up, shrieking. He dropped his gun with a wet sound, slapping frantically at a growing sea of fire that spread across his back, melting his skin to the latex of the uniform. Two women, both new additions to the personal guard, met similar fates, squealing as they were burned alive, charred black in front of the rest.

Horrific resolve set in amongst her security force as they quickly withdrew to the emergency stairwells at the rear of the room closing the doors and locking them. For a few seconds, the only sound was laboured breathing; Huntress did a quick headcount and came out with twenty five or so. Probably about the same number in the other stairwell, she surmised. Half of her guard was dead.

The first of the trucks exploded, the gas tank rupturing and throwing metal in each direction, setting off a chain reaction. Like the footfalls of titans shaking the very mantle of the Earth, everything seemed to shake and reverberate. The noise was deafening; The Huntress had implants to reduce the damage caused from the sonic boom. The blast ruptured eardrums and rendered some fully unconscious, unable to take the pain. Blood gushed from the ears of an older guard standing just to the left of the door; he slumped with a quiet dignity into a near-unconscious crouch. He still kept his grip firm on his weapon; Huntress felt a note of silent approval. Not many of the best pulled from the last few classes had shown such mettle. The door had been blown nearly clear of its hinges, wrenched by the terrific force of the explosions so that was jammed ajar, one corner buried in the steel grating of the emergency stairs within.

"Now!" she urged, kicking the heavy door free with a strength beyond any of them. It tumbled end over end before striking the carcass of a truck with a bang, her forces spilling back out into the lobby with weapons at the ready.

The Eldritch were waiting for them, along with what Gears remained. Zip guns, poached pistols, and a few rifles peppered the doorways as the security forces spilled out. The first few through the door bore the brunt of the poorly trained attackers, torn apart by bullets they'd never seen coming. Some slumped in the threshold, slowing the Huntress and her elite guard as they reclaimed the lobby. Their guns were full and the hands holding them trained, they emptied them into the rebels without pause. The madmen and the greasers were cut down where they stood, some throwing down their cheap hardware and rushing to melee.

Huntress moved forward to greet them, pulling her twin kukri from her belt and challenging a nearby Eldritch to rush her, a long steel pipe in his hands. Clumsily he gave a battlecry and attempted a crushing blow towards her leading leg. She quickly darted back, then rushed in and drove both machetes into his gut, drawing the curved blade upward and opening his stomach wide. His whimpering pleas as he struggled with his innards were joined by the high shriek of engines. As the gang member flopped facedown beside her, clutching the knives in his stomach and croaking his last, The Huntress saw something unbelievable. Blazing fast, whipping between the husks of the trucks with ease, black clad murderers in their midst. They leapt from their bikes, allowing the heavy iron horses to tumble free and smash into the thick knots of confused and tired security officers, slaying many outright as their weak flesh was entangled and broken. Swords sprang free from scabbards and the Killers fell upon their enemies, the security forces fighting back with flagging strength.

Huntress sat in a stupor; the battle seemed to unfold about her as she crouched in cover, hand resting against the depleted siding of a truck. This had to be something more than a random act of terror. There had to be a goal. Peering over the scene, eyes flitting from struggle to struggle, she saw life and death dance in her bright blue eyes. Then she saw her. And him.

Her costume was a retro looking leather. Almost as tall as The Huntress, not quite as muscular. The same flat, deadly stare. She gripped a Beretta in her fist and was speaking frantically with a man as tall as she, and twice as wide. A man she recognized immediately.

The Mountain. The Huntress could not help but feel her mouth make an *o* of surprise at the sight. His frame, once hewn from rock, gave way to a softness about the middle that tugged at the buttons of his white dress shirt. His iconic black suit and ponytail could not be mistaken. He nodded in reply, only opening his mouth to offer a single word. They parted ways, the big man making a quick exit towards the emergency elevator that Huntress had propped open, the woman in red squeezing under the railing and then slinking up to the emergency stairwell to the right.

Meanwhile, war raged on in the lobby. It was now a hand to hand affair, flashing blades and the grunts and grounds of lethal combat filling the air. The Killers time in the kwoon and on the streets had paid off, they were at least a match for the well-trained Elite, using their unorthodox tactics to great effect despite being outnumbered. The odd Eldritch standing would dart into a conflict, stabbing a knife between exposed ribs and fading away, or lit for an instant against the black powder explosion of a found weapon pulled from a dead man. Men and women fell, stabbing and beating one another, cursing each other into oblivion.

The Huntress stood and immediately sprang into action, sprinting across the empty space separating her from a group of soldiers who had taken cover behind a trio of trashed motorcycles. They were taking sparing potshots overtop, hoping to score a lucky hit without exposing themselves. The Huntress fell into a controlled slide and pulled herself around the obstacle, kneeling.

"You five. Up that stairwell. You're no good to me hiding here." She nodded at the right-hand stairwell. "She's going after the catalyst."

The troop leader, a stern faced young woman with a square cut jaw and small, mean eyes nodded her understanding and ordered it so. Keeping low, service pistols at the ready, they juked between cover towards the landing. With nearly forty floors to go, they'd catch her.

The Huntress had her own destiny, handed to her as if by fate. Legs pumping beneath her, she ran towards the left stairwell, abandoned and far from the action that was raging in the lobby. There were no more shots ringing out now, ammunition expended and empty guns scattered on the floor, bodies wrestling, struggling for their lives.

"The molotov cocktails burst, ravenous flames shooting across the carpeted floor, up the walls..."

Illustration by Jesse H. Walker.

CHAPTER 9: STAIRWAY TO HELL

On the twenty-fourth floor, Domina first felt the fear of failure. She wasn't going to make it. Her left arm hung limp, useless, an early shot from below had winged her and spun her hard against the uneven metal stairs. It hurt to breathe too deeply – a second shot somewhere around the tenth floor had caught her square in the back, the sewn kevlar weave beneath the quilted lining of her jacket the only reason she was still alive. She gasped, air coming ragged and shallow. Weak white emergency lights, some barely working, offered the only illumination on the steel staircase.

She'd killed one who got too close. It was the same bastard who shot her in the back. A little to eager for the kill, he'd leapt the stairs two at a time looking for some easy glory. Thinking the girl was hurt worse than she was. His last mistake. She rolled onto her back and blasted him with the Beretta, driving a slug through his forehead. The muzzle flash captured a surprised look as he fell away, rolling down the stairs. She'd scrambled on hands and knees until she'd managed to start climbing again, her hunters in hot pursuit.

Domina could not run any further. She doubled over and hacked violently, tasting familiar iron in her mouth. Her lungs heaved, desperate for oxygen. She spit and crouched, gripping her Beretta and trailing her attackers. Grouped together, she pulled the trigger twice as they reached the landing two flights below. Cries of alarm arose. One unlucky guardswoman took a round above the breastplate, through the collarbone, and she was pinned hard to the ground. Two of her companions knelt beside her, checking vitals, as another popped a round back to provide cover.

Domina shrugged away as the bullet rang far distant. She had an ideal angle while the troop below held a very poor one. Refusing to be cowed, she leaned overtop the floor of her landing, aimed, and sent two more rounds hailing down upon them. One caught the guardsmen kneeling to check the vitals of his downed comrade just above the ear, drilling a perfect circle, pushing him into a still and awkward pose in the corner.

A scream of rage and frustration echoed against the steel

corridor from below as the remaining security men lost themselves to unfamiliar emotion, primal and bestial. Recklessly rushing up the stairs, they came at her, teeth bared in feral, animal anger. They discharged the few rounds they had left as soon as they caught sight of her, spraying the walls about her but doing little damage. They hurled the useless hunks of metal at her, forcing her to duck as they closed to mere meters.

The thick steel grating vibrated beneath their boots as they closed with her. Domina leveled the Beretta and pulled the trigger as the three guardsmen crested the staircase, joining her on the landing. Her last two bullets barked from the barrel, both taking the man high in the chest. He cartwheeled from the landing, striking the stairwell hard many flights down.

The two men that were facing her now could not be more different, though both wore murder on their faces. One was dark, exotic in appearance, with deep brown eyes and curly hair. The other, thinner and more gaunt, appeared almost a ghost, doe-eyed and soft-featured. Both gripped standard issue combat knives in their hands.

158

Domina holstered her gun and drew her machete. Her father had given it to her long ago. *The machete is more than a weapon. The machete is a noble tool. Many people have lived by this blade alone.* She smiled at his wisdom as the sharpened blade snicked free of its scabbard. She would honour her father.

The three of them danced, circling one another, twin snakes pressing her for advantage and her never giving quarter, leaping forward to meet them, naked steel in her fist. The man with the soft face pressed advantage first, coming in low, looking for an opportunity to put his knife in her soft belly. He was too slow, her machete arced down upon the nape of his neck and separated head from shoulders. Legs collapsed and the body slipped free and over the lip of the landing, head looping end over end into the darkness.

Domina and the lone guardsman, slowly pacing one another, blades extended. The heels of their boots rang out against the corrugated steel grating. The echoes were unearthly, like chimes out of tune.

"You don't have to die, you know. Leave," she said. She

was serious. "I'll let you live."

He laughed, a dark gleam in his gaze. "I don't trust you, bitch. You killed my friends. I won't let you live."

"They had it coming."

"*You* have it coming!"

Raising a battlecry, the swarthy man rushed forward; Domina dropped her weight and prepared to sidestep. It was a feint. Her opponent darted left and slashed a deep furrow across her exposed thigh, cutting through her combat pants. She swung wildly but he had already ducked away, again circling her as clutched at her leg with her free hand.

He quickly shifted in, knife held by his hips for a stabbing motion, capitalizing on her pain and distraction. Catching his hand between her hip and arm, she slashed at his captive arm, nearly cutting it free. Arterial spray coated her, adding a new shade to her leather, strands of muscle and ligament giving way as the man's dead weight pulled him backwards. His arm fell loose and dropped heavily to the landing. His screams were short-lived as his lifeblood poured out, through the grate, dripping into the blackness below. He died within seconds, three stairs down.

She checked their pockets, quickly. Tossed the wallets and snack wrappers; kept the keycard IDs. Only one of them was holding any ammo, a used 9mm magazine with just two rounds left. Two rounds were better than none. She reloaded her weapon, switching mags with the dead soldier.

Holding one hand hard against the deep gash in her leg to help staunch the wound, the other gripping the railing. The blade of the machete slapped the rail as she hobbled up the stairs. She reached the 34th floor before blacking out.

CHAPTER 10: RETURN TO THE DAO

The Mountain emerged from the elevator on the thirtieth floor with a sense of trepidation, alert. The pinnacle was on the fortieth floor, the floor he had selected when he'd gotten in. Somebody had obviously shorted out access to the higher floors. The fortieth floor was famously the apex, the pinnacle.

The lights were dimmed in the hallway; a quick look to the left and the right revealed no obvious threats. He stepped out of the elevator, knelt and used a nearby flowerpot to wedge the sliding doors. It would prop them open for some light, keep his supplies handy, and keep the elevator locked and ready on this floor.

Then he heard the sound of singing. It was muffled, but not that far. Inside a room down the hallway to the left. He followed the sweet notes, almost operatic, wondering why they sounded so familiar. Comprehension grew as The Mountain realized it was the same performer who had been singing during the Mouth's newscast earlier this evening!

Of course, the broadcast studios would be located here, in the house of the Elite. Consolidate power, keep communications close to your chest so they can be more easily controlled. Was this singer friend or foe, hostage or ally? Thoughts ran through his head and he compartmentalized them, gently pushing them away from his senses. Reaching the end of the hallway, he again peeked about the corner. The singing was much louder now, more forceful, almost as if created for the purpose of calling him to battle.

It was coming from a door around the bend at the end of the hallway, a fake potted plant standing tall and proud beside the door marked "Primary studio / soundstage." He crept low to the ground, closer to the door. It was ajar; that's why the singing had been so loud. All of his senses told him it was a trap. Warily, he lightly kicked open the door, which swung wide on smooth hinges.

The singing grew louder, almost immediate. He could tell that she was no more than a forty or fifty feet away, behind the small reception area that confronted him. A small alcove to the left, a kitchenette. Two short, modern looking chairs and a coffee percolator. More fake foliage, though not cheap, crept along the lines of the room like ivy – an unusual and esoteric touch of decor.

His broadsword held close, he stayed low to the ground and made his way through the small warming area, towards an archway which led to what he presumed was the actual studio. The lights were on; he could see that much, though they had been dimmed.

Her song was sad, very different from the one he'd seen on the stream earlier, though he knew it to be the same voice. Tremulous at times, a mournful timbre inflected every tone. He tried not to allow it to distract him as he peered around the corner, hoping to get a better look inside the room.

Stars exploded in front of his eyes as he was struck a heavy blow. Reeling in surprise, The Mountain windmilled backwards, falling stunned in the far corner of the studio. Before he could gain his wits, his assailant had closed with him again, chopping at his hand with a crushing strength, disarming him, the sword spinning away. He felt himself lifted into the air like a ragdoll, despite his great bulk, and hurled. He landed heavily in the midst of the room, the hardwood of the studio floor doing little to break the fall.

The singing stopped abruptly. Sirenia opened her eyes in surprise. The Mouth motioned for the droids to get her out of there. Her work was done. He, himself, remained seated behind the cherrywood desk, a silent observer. Sirenia felt herself gently clasped by the wrist, the dwarfish android looking up almost expectantly at her. Time to leave. Sirenia stepped over the hulking form, giving one last sad look over her shoulder as she disappeared into the kitchenette and was gone. A replacement robot wheeled over on rubber tracks and began displaying its own red light, taking over camera duty. The stream focused first on the handsome face of Alan Scarlet.

"Take your time with him. Our viewers are reporting extreme pleasure at the proceedings. The show must go on," The Mouth urged The Huntress, his usual professional amiability coloured by something more perverse, some deep-seated personal pleasure.

The Huntress nodded, the tall blonde taking the time to

survey the old man gathering his balance, pushing his way to a precarious standing position. How could she work with this? There was nothing left to destroy. She'd just have to get a little more creative in her approach to humiliation.

His leg was encased in an inferior looking servo rig, probably put together by a chop shop; she'd seen the match and wasn't surprised by the augmentation.

"So. The Mountain. The Legend. Master of the Old Ways. Stoops so low as to use a gimmick to help him stand?"

He saw her, then, for the first time up close. Exceptionally tall, taller than he. Long, lustrous blonde hair — natural. Not a shred of evidence of sweat or exertion. Her pure white garments had been stained a variety of gruesome hues, however, marring the archetype of perfection and lending him confidence. She spread her arms wide as she circled him. He kept his eyes pinned to her, watching for the sign that signaled her move.

"Don't be afraid!" she cooed as a mother to a child, a nurse to an invalid, taunting. "I'm unarmed."

They both knew that The Huntress did not need

weaponry, her superior genetic profile and training meant that she was one of the physically strongest people alive. If anything, it was a chill reminder to The Mountain that he, too, was unarmed.

"You're nothing but a washed up old man, an example of what happens when you live in the past instead of the present."

"The past has many lessons for us in the present. The past allows us to perceive the future. This basic truth is obscured from you. You wear a veil at all hours and delight in the colour of it before your face, never having the courage to remove it. Not even once. You are a coward. As I was."

"A coward?" Huntress sneered cruelly. With speed beyond reckoning and a viciousness fueled by spite, she brought an armored fist down across The Mountain's crippled leg. The snap of servos, steel, and bone was audible; the big man staggered under his great weight, eventually falling to both knees. "A coward?" she leaned into the crook of his neck, breathing hot, cooing the words.

She gripped his ponytail and rained blows down upon

his face, blackening his eyes, breaking a cheekbone, flattening his nose.

He remained mute, except for the wheezing gasps and gurgles he made in an effort to breath, remaining upright as a mess ran down his jaw and chest. She ripped his shirt open, revealing a chest made soft by the years. Knots of muscle, aging and tired, under a thick layer of fat.

"This?!" The Huntress laughed derisively, "the legend I was to compare myself to? An out of shape cripple? What a sick joke."

An inhuman sound like the laughter of the devil came forth from between The Mountain's swollen lips and tongue.

"You think this is a joke? Let me show you something before you die. Something to amuse us both."

The Huntress left his side, unclenching her fist from around his ponytail, letting him slump freely. He refused to sag, shuddering, feeling his body protest, wanting to collapse and perhaps lie there forever. He could not see well enough to tell where she had gone. She returned quickly, pressing something into his hand, cupping his ear and hissing: "The joke is everything you stand for. The ancient ways that have betrayed you at every turn. Led you down the path of a failure. Time to laugh grandpa."

She pushed him away. He tripped and fell heavily on his bad leg. The Huntress laughed, clapping gleefully.

"Oh come now! Weren't you rated at 12.8 standards? *The man can barely stand!*" she cried out theatrically. The Mountain used his sword to help him gain footing, still looking very shaky and unable to put any weight on his bad leg.

"That was a long time ago, when I was like you," he said through swollen lips.

"Like me? Younger, you mean. Stronger. Vital."

"No. Not that. More easily led. Impressionable. Selfish. All myopic traits for mortals. Shortsighted. My eyes were opened. I see the Dao, the taijitu. Yin, yang. Light and darkness. You are blind to the shadows. As I was. Long before I shamed myself by fighting for money. For pride. For glory. Three fatal illusions," he slurred, barely able to see, his head lolling.

"Spare me the mystical nonsense. Time to end this — in

front of the world. At least die with dignity."

The Huntress said dismissively, rushing at him with sword at the ready. She was the embodiment of a cruel and vicious beauty, smiling crookedly even as she came to kill him. Her longer sword lashed out, battering his blade aside. She sought to run him through. She barely saw him move — did *not* see the sai slip into his palm from the cuff of his suit. Did not see the rigidity return to his frame, the whipcord of long forgotten muscle memory coming to attention. A jarring impact as the stout sai stopped her katana cold, catching the tip between the tines. Shock spread over her expression as she clinched with The Mountain. They crashed together, neither budging, her armor bruising his already tender flesh.

For the first time in her life, The Huntress felt pain. Howling, gnashing, spewing froth, she wriggled. The Chinese broadsword burst from her back, protruding from a messy wound. A ragged panel hung loose from her armor, the elaborate lines of the plating ran red.

"Save us! Oh, save us!" Alan Scarlet shouted in dramatic horror, overheard and echoed by those watching the stream as the camera remained fixed on the grisly scene.

The Mountain lifted her from the ground, the blade cutting even deeper into her organs. Blood pooled in an ever expanding circle beneath her high boots, dripping from the heels. Her beautiful blonde hair fell to mask most of her face. She opened her eyes to stare into the ruined face of her killer.

The Huntress gurgled, trying to form words. Pink bubbles ran freely from her painted lips. "What? How?" Pure disbelief was reflected in her eyes. Death was for others. Suffering was for others. Theoretical and far removed. Immediacy of both made her a child. She tried to spit in his face but could not muster one last breath.

"Just because you do not see what lurks within the shadows does not make them less substantial. Perception is not reality. In death, we learn the most important lessons. This lesson may teach you some humility in your next life."

She expired quickly on his sword, spasming to the last. The camera caught it all and streamed it all. Every last word whispered, the dying embers in The Huntress' eyes. The robotic crew in Post-processing had meticulously and artistically framed each moment of the struggle, the climax, the anticlimax as The Mountain pushed the corpse from his blade and wiped it clean on the legs of his cheap black suit before sheathing it. He tore the wrecked rigging of the servo from his bad leg and cast it off.

Wordlessly, he turned his back on the corpse as he slid the small sai back under his cuff. Limping towards the stairs, The Mountain did not even deign to ask for forgiveness for the life he had taken. He did not even turn to address The Mouth, Alan Scarlet, still seated in absolute shock and disbelief at his desk, fearful to move. His shadow side was rising and a sense of fatality accompanied it as he painstakingly hobbled up the stairs, towards the pinnacle of the Spire where the Sufferer slept.

The robotic camera operator did not move to follow, merely turning its unblinking red eye on a swivel to gaze upon The Mouth, drained of all colour.

CHAPTER 11: SIMON AND THE DRONES

The melee raged on in the lobby below, the remnants of the massacre fighting at a fevered pitch. The drones had swept into the lobby to assist the remaining Killers, vastly outnumbered by the increasingly confident security forces. Turncoat had taken cover behind the metal hulk of a downed motorcycle, prone, taking potshots with a pistol he'd stolen from a dead guard. His ammo was running dangerously low and he'd already been wounded once, winged in the left arm. Good thing his right was his good arm. Fear coursed through him.

The drone pilots were in a basement, far away, underground. Each of them was strapped into an optical headset, tactile controls strapped to their fingers so that they could use the HUD to pilot their cheap drones. More than half of rebels sat silent, their headsets off and held between their knees. Some of them were whispering to themselves, soft reassurances or prayers. The rest were entranced, immersed in their task.

Lill piloted the lead drone, the only one with a full gun attached. She'd taken out three of the bastards so far, stitching bullets across their backs when they were otherwise occupied, employing hit and run tactics. She buzzed in and out of cover, drawing fire away from her allies, seeing a few of her wingmates clipped from the sky, detonating recklessly below, mutilating those nearby. She saw Turncoat cower against the broken frame of the bike as bullets whined and sparked against the chrome next to his head. She felt at least some stirring of pride when he had the courage to throw his good arm overtop and pop a few errant return shots off.

The sunset orange of her HUD washed over her eyes, she could see a framework of her fingers interacting with the immaterial controls. They were losing the battle, and would be overrun eventually. That meant they had a new mission: last as long as possible; buy enough time for the others; send the signal to scatter for those pilots already downed. She tapped absently at a tertiary panel on the HUD and the latter order was given. Lill heard the sound of metal chair legs scraping against the floor, as if from far away. Despite the short notice, the Scholars had been well organized and, removed from the action, subject to less immediate stress.

Lill felt no such inner peace as she wrestled with her drone, swinging it wildly through the air to avoid concentrated gunfire by two guards which had spotted her. Their aim was wide and only a single round struck the drone, deflecting harmlessly.

The same guards then took aim at another drone buzzing in Lill's wake. Their shots tore through the winged weapon; it tumbled to the ground and rolled clear of the warzone before exploding to little effect.

Then she saw Simon flinch, cringing tight against cover, as a new assault found him and struck out at him. Four guardsmen, having finished off their enemies, converged on his hiding spot. Without hesitation, Lill swept from the shadows, buzzing at full speed towards the group, unleashing the remaining half-clip she had in store.

The small calibre automatic fire caught one soldier in the legs and chest, thrusting him earthward. The rest of the barrage missed, and Lill swung her drone low and fast in order to use crossfire to her advantage. In a panic, the guardsmen on opposite sides of the lobby shot at the streaking drone, missing entirely, some stray bullets catching one another. Furious cries bit the night air, a ragged and defeated laugh came from the few Killers left standing, knee deep in the dead.

Turncoat turned and rose to a crouch, hooting in celebration and firing his last few rounds into the last man standing, facing him down. The hammer came down empty. He had only a moment of extreme confusion before he felt the hammerblow of a bullet slamming into his own chest, twisting his torso, throwing him hard to the ground. He had no time to register fear before it was over for him.

It was revenge that motivated her to drive the steel-winged drone into an immediate nosedive as she looped around a bullet-ridden column, whipping around the post, careening kamikaze onto the soldier who had shot Simon. She had never called him by his codename, considering it too plain an insult for too sensitive a man.

Her HUD disappeared as the drone detonated on impact, surely ending the life of the guardsman. There was no longer the chatter of gunfire, nor the tormented screams of the injured and the dying. There was only the low noise of the cooling fan keeping her rig operational, and even this was entering automatic shutdown and format. Wipe it all clean.

Lill removed her headset, pulling it away with a wet suction. She blinked owlishly, the fluorescent lighting above a stark contrast to the digital immersion. She wiped at her brow; it felt clammy and damp. She was alone, the last one left in the makeshift operations room. Cables ran across the floors, walls, and ceilings, intertwined and strung together randomly in a messy rat's nest.

The computer banks remained silent, a few stragglers still spinning their fans and grinding out the last few bytes into oblivion, scrubbing the hard disks clean and then initiating a terminal error. Lill gathered her backpack, flipped the display switch next to the tower back to the monitor to see how the format was coming along. Forty-two percent with ten minutes remaining

Lill allowed the seconds to pass, the blue bar on the monitor rising ever so slowly. Proper destruction took time. The sweeper team would be by in ten or twenty minutes to torch the place. Minutes later, as the progress bar inched well past the halfway mark, she rose from her metal folding chair and abandoned the basement, seeking the safety of the shadows and the confusion of the crowd. The door at the end of the stairs leading from the basement opened into a back alley in the entertainment district. Drunken, animal panic reigned in the streets; it was total chaos as personalities and motives clashed. Arguments, fights, voices raised in alarm and confusion backgrounded by the wail of enforcement vehicles speeding to quell a potential riot.

Lill pulled her knitted hat low over her ears, pulled the collar of her peacoat tight against the nape of her neck, and calmly wandered down the alleyway in the opposite direction, away from the human host, away from the multicoloured storefronts and onstreet patios, swelling with revelers — some too intoxicated to even realize there was an emergency. The cacophony, the noise that set her teeth on edge, receded with each step she took into the unlit passage leading elsewhere.

She thought of Simon — sensitive Simon who'd brought them the key to everything, the only artifact of reason that might survive the madness of tonight — and how quickly his defiant flame had been snuffed out. She thought of her father and wondered if he still lived.

CHAPTER 12: THE SUFFERER

He'd carried her as far as he could, despite his destroyed leg and grievous injuries. Now, he was spent, all energy gone, body depleted and perhaps never to rise again.

The Mountain lowered the unconscious woman to the ground, then fell heavily beside her, wheezing and sucking for air. He allowed himself the self-pity of allowing a low moan to pass his lips.

Her eyelids fluttered; Domina saw the world as a blurry nothingness, small lights through an ashy grime. She struggled towards consciousness. Her fingers clenched, gripping steel grating beneath her. Of course – a landing. The fireflies floating above – emergency lights. She remembered. Her fingertips ran the length of her body; they felt the touch of a tourniquet tying off her wounded leg. She could not feel her leg. Domina locked that particular panic away, someplace deep in her mind, fighting to forget. Her mind latched onto more pressing matters.

"Mountain? My friend?" she rasped. Her mouth felt dry as a desert, her voice was paper-thin.

"I am here, Domina. Though not for much longer," he said in his same low voice. She turned her head to look at him. His golden skin was beaten black and blue, his lips puffed and both eyes nearly shut. He was barely recognizable. He was dying. Her heart broke. She twitched on the floor as emotion stole over her, her discipline failing.

"You're hurt! You shouldn't have carried me! You overdid it!" she was beyond herself.

"You needed help. Nothing could have stopped this, dearest friend. You have been like a sister to Lill, a daughter to me. These past few months..." he attempted a smile, the result was macabre, "have brought me peace. I have you to thank for bringing me back to the Dao. Never forget the love I held for you. Watch over your sister."

Slowly, with a badly shaking hand, he reached clumsily between the folds of his blazer, going for the breast pocket. Lacking the strength. His arm went slack.

The big man convulsed once, then his head slung down upon his broad chest. His heart, tortured too long, stopped.

There was a slight rattle from his lungs. He slumped over, gently, at rest. His black suit betrayed nothing, torn in so many places yet still managing to look distinguished, even though his face was a battered mess of indignity. Death did not care for beauty or ugliness, it stole upon him and detached his soul from his body. Domina held him until he began to stiffen, shaking with emotion.

Then, tearing its way up from her lungs, rushing through her throat and exploding outward, her primal fury. Louder, angrier, a red haze settled over her vision, filling her muscles with strength and causing her chest to heave. Power filled her, a gift. Her inhuman cry continued as long as her lungs would bear, drained and deflated. She snorted, rising to her feet and clenching her fists so hard that they bled, fingernails tearing into the flesh of her palms.

She knelt beside The Mountain's body, and with ironic gentleness unfolded his arms, laying him on his back in repose. She reached into his breast pocket and felt reassuring steel. A small pistol was what she pulled free, plain and black. The safety was still on and the magazine was full. It hadn't been fired in years.

There were no more stairs to climb. The emergency lights above were pointed towards a dull red steel door with a reinforced glass pane window. The door was locked. Domina balled her fist and struck the window as hard as she could. The first blow shattered the glass into the reinforcement mesh, the second and third blows loosened the metal netting, the fourth punch broke through. She did not feel the pain. Reality was remote, shards of glass and metal shavings slicing through her gloves and skin, burying bits in her knuckles. She did not hear any footfalls, no echoing clang of boots on the ascent, but she knew they would come and that time was of the essence.

Reaching through the small window and around to the latch, Domina unlocked the door and slipped through, locking it behind her. She found herself in a long hallway, elegantly decorated. The emergency lighting fell upon priceless works of art absconded from the rubble of the ancients; some prints she'd recognized from old vids and books. There did not appear to be any common theme other than exceptional beauty, whether landscape or portraiture or abstraction. The hallway of art led towards a singular chamber which, even as she approached it, Domina could tell was the pinnacle of the Spire. It was the sleeping chambers of The Sufferer. She gripped the pistol in her right hand, her left throbbing, broken.

She emerged into the high-vaulted chamber, gun at the ready. A single figure occupied the room with her, tall and thin and wearing the embroidered black labcoat of The Watcher. He was an Elite scientist, the most intelligent man living. Surely he was not sitting idle, nor easy prey.

Beyond him, an enclosure, the highest point, the rear of the room. A rough stairwell lead up to it. Sealed off by thick glass, a high-tech looking door with a keypad was the only way in or out. A lone prisoner was seated precisely in the middle of the floor. Behind him was the legendary tree of tears, the only tree of its species, the first tree ever brought back by one of of the scavenging worms that the earliest men sent to the surface. It was a vibrant, vital green, emerald in colour, with buds the colour of snow and sapphires. The boughs were strong and knobby, the needles long and thin and delicate. Many had fallen to criss-cross the simple stone floor of The Sufferer's cell, some rested on his shabby outfit or were entwined with his long, white beard.

The Sufferer himself was as a statue, hard to deem living if it weren't for the healthy bloom of his flesh.

The Watcher made no quick movements, his fingers interlocked and held in his lap as he walked slowly forward, allowing what little light was left in the chamber to show his face to her. He was middle aged, had delicate features, thick glasses, and a sour looking expression of the habitually unsatisfied and underserved.

"So. An illegal. I never thought it would be one of our own kind that was leading this idiotic crusade and I'm glad I was right. Though I am ashamed that so many of us did aide you, though they are almost all certainly dead or in detention at this point."

"How did you know? You can't see my back."

"Can't I? I scanned you the moment you began climbing the stairwell. Not that it did much good, seeing as how you are not a person."

Domina laughed, then, though she did not close her eyes or take her pistol from the position she had brought it to bear. It was pinned to The Watcher's heart, unwavering. Her laughter was cruel, short, without humour.

184

"You're a dead man. You are not a person." Her every word dripped with venom. Hatred.

"So, you want to be a hero?" He ignored the threat, taking another few steps closer. They were now less than ten feet apart. "To save the rest of us? To show us how righteous you are? How your pain and suffering makes you stronger? Learn from his example, then!" The Watcher pointed an accusing finger at The Sufferer. Domina darted a glance over The Watcher's shoulder at the decrepit figure, stock still in his menagerie. The Watcher glimpsed this momentary flicker of attention away from his eyes. She saw the rising intent in the scientist's gaze.

"Surely you know this plan will fail. Anarchy will result. We have created a new Eden, free of pain and negativity and struggle and anxiety. You would return us to fear? Many would die," he said to her.

"You are all already dead. And you killed many of my friends. You took my family away from me when I was just a little girl. Then you tried to seduce me, condition me, tell me that it was right and just. All lies."

"I see for The Sufferer. I represent his wishes. There

185

must be another catalyst. All of your personal problems don't amount to a trifle against these realities of our society. Do you not understand that we require him to live? Without him, we are diminished. And I am the only one who can speak for him. He does not speak to you, I know this for certain."

"You blind fool! Your conduit is one way; you are unable to see as he does. I see for The Sufferer, for I am one. My pain brings me closer to the fearful, the sick, the weak — to him!" she cried out passionately, forgetting herself.

The Watcher gave a noise of disgust. He raised both hands slowly to show he was unarmed, then tapped a brooch on his lapel. A chirping noise was the response, and audio slowly filled the room from invisible speakers. It was a noise of the crowd, stirred to bloodlust.

"*This* is your heroism? Do you realize how many people died tonight?"

"Many. Many of them were my friends. My only family. I cared for them in ways that people like you never will. You understand nothing but rhetoric. You twist the words to suit your purpose but you don't hear them in your heart.

When one of my friends dies, I feel it. Let me show you what hate can achieve."

Domina pulled the trigger, the small snap of the .22 round drowned out by the chorus of voices pouring forth from the audio stream. The Watcher took the round neatly through his left eye. There was no exit wound, he merely fell dead away, sprawled across the wide-hewn stone steps leading to The Sufferer's prison. His great mind gone in an instant, ephemeral.

"He is a hero," Domina said as she slowly walked over his body, favouring her good leg. "I wish I could show you that, too."

Domina raised the pistol and pumped every remaining round into the glass jar encapsulating the catalyst. Each round struck home and shattered glass, some bouncing off and some remaining lodged. Irregular etchings, splayed over the surface, spiderwebs that formed deep cracks. The voices that had begun to whisper and roar as The Watcher had tapped his lapel had not ceased; it was actually growing in intensity. They must be drawing nearer, seeking the source of their troubles, answers to the mysteries that had obscured their understandings. It was the rumble of uncertainty, and it caused a deep thrumming vibration throughout the pinnacle chamber.

The glass creaked, edges biting together and grinding. Then a piece fell loose and free, then another. With one more well-placed blast from the .22 pistol, a great piece of glass shattered, the stress too great. The hole was barely large enough for Domina to squeeze through; the ragged edges cut into her leather and left marks all over her as she wriggled into the cell with the catalyst.

She fell inside gracelessly, landing on her bad shoulder and driving a spike of pain up her arm that brought more explosive curses to her lips. Throughout it all, staggering to her feet, she saw no sign of awareness from The Sufferer, silent beneath his tree.

As the tension in the voices climbed higher and higher towards apex, her inner turmoil was doused with each step she gained closer to the catalyst. She stood next to him, looked down upon his bent, stoic frame. She felt a connection to him. An unspeakable, intangible bond. Something spiritual.

His skin appeared old, but not ancient. Lined from stress and a harsh life, scars wound their way about his head, neck, and shoulders — from battle, not from disease. His was a body that had been abused for a lifetime, and was now slowly fading away. He wore no clothing, his nudity asexual, ascetic. He had been strong, once. He was still a fighter. He had lasted longer than anyone who came before him.

She would see that none would come after, or ever again. There would be no more Sufferer. She could not wait. It had to end now.

She knelt beside him. She reached out to feel for his pulse. A turgid, slow, strong heartbeat was present, rolling over only once every few long seconds. Still, he showed no sign of sensing her presence.

Domina embraced him, moving her broken hand behind his bony back, feeling his vertebrae rubbing against the bones of her forearm as she gripped him steadily.

The view was breath-taking. If The Sufferer had opened his eyes he could see the whole cavern city laid out before him. Brightly-lit streets filled with the forms of people; a solid mob, like ants, pouring down the megapass towards the spire. Fires burned at various points in the city. It was beginning already. It was too late to stop now.

She raised the pistol to the Sufferer's chest, pressing the warm barrel against his left breast.

"I'm so sorry," she whispered to him, her emotions coloured every word as looking into his wizened, familiar features.

She pulled the trigger as he opened his eyes in reply, bright green irises speaking love in return.

PROLOGUE: THE COAL WORM

When they'd caught him, he was crying. A sure sign of feedback sickness. Emotional overflow. Panic. Reasons he could not reveal, even to himself, upon pain of torture or drugged manipulation.

Ignorance may not be bliss, but it was far less dangerous for her. For *them*.

By the time that they'd first suited him up in his stark white outfit, he could barely remember anything. He was entirely dissociative, floating above his body, his consciousness attached by visible strings. Visible to his mind and as invisible to others.

That had been years ago, now. He couldn't count how many, and it didn't really seem to matter in any case.

He'd gone to the surface a few times for them now. How long ago had he been abducted from his home? Strangled in his sleep and beaten savagely under a circle of cruel faces. The memory caused a thrill of fear to shoot up his spine.

The Coal Worm clenched his teeth, grinding them, pushing it *down*. To display anger would mean certain death; for his mind and his soul if not his meat, his body.

They clothed him in the garb of a coal worm for the fifth time. It was rare that a surface subject — a worm that went all the way to the surface on each expedition — survived past their second assignment. No matter how many times they had reinstalled the shunt and played with its firmware, he would never distribute emotional stream, only accept it. When interrogated, the coal worm in question inevitably indicated that he had no idea why the shunt would not function; he denied making any alterations to the device and this claim was borne out by microscoping scan.

So they rerouted his shunt, disconnecting him. Leaving him individuated by force.

He was doomed to his fate. This was a demonstration of their total control.

The guardsmen handling him clad him in white and sent the Coal Worm to the surface, as often as his body would bear. Each time he returned, broken and battered and covered in black, spending weeks and often months in convalescence as he healed from the burn and the wounds.

This time they told him that they did not expect him to survive. Reports from the surface panels showed that three arrays needed light to moderate repair, in various parts of the city-above. There was simply not enough manpower, what with all of the losses lately. What his bosses meant were deaths. They needed him. He was given his orders.

They told him this with what posed as regret, their faces pulled long in impersonation.

It was the same shit every time. This time, however, he faced trials equivalent to a death sentence.

The Coal Worm was clamped onto the Prime stalactite, the one which hovered over the university which bore its name. The shortest route to the surface was the airway which had been their original path downward into the safety of the cavern, an ancient natural exit.

He held the hooks in his hands. They were wrapped around his wrist with leather and chains, and could gut a man as well as dig deep into the soft rock of the cavern. Spiked boots gave him his footing.

He began his ascent. Hand over hand, feeling the metal bite hard, lifting himself up on straining muscles. He did not look down; his mind's eye provided a portrait panoramic. The small stone humps of humble dwellings crowding around the more angular, industrial splines of the market buildings, commercial spaces. The Spire, House of the Elites, a proud finger emerging from the ground yet still far short of meeting the Prime stalactite.

He knew the lights from below were there, could see their glow against the soot and against his own white suit. Yet he never looked back.

It was a brutal journey. He pulled himself upward for hours, the light of the city fading away at the end of a constricting tunnel.

He encountered the corpse nets, laden with the burden of dead flesh. Protruding at odd angles on rough iron spokes, thick rope strung between them, wrapped in razor wire. The odd abomination from the surface, unknowable and unnameable horrors to those who dwelt below, would tumble down the shafts no matter how well concealed or partitioned. The nets were a sluice, catching almost all of the twisted forms before they could splash and burst upon the cavern floor. Most of them were empty, but some held writhing, wriggling bounty. He had stabbed his hooks viciously and repeatedly into each such net as he passed until they lie still and silent.

The first rest station was like something given to him by God, if the Coal Worm had such notions. He did not. Sprawled out on the flat ledge hewn into the side of the airway like a giant's sconce, he writhed on his stomach. He convulsed, his muscles in spasm. He moaned and cried out to nobody and nothing.

After several long moments, he regained his wits and cast about for the kit. A white plastic box was screwed into the stone wall. He opened it to reveal the dose. He loaded the syringe, pulling a double dose from a bottle of amber liquid. He found a vein, held the needle to his skin, felt it bite him. Pressed the plunger, felt a cool sensation flow through his arm and into his heart.

He felt warm. He felt strong. He pulled the needle free and stared at the small bead of blood springing forth, pooling then running. He heard it run to the floor in a pitter patter. No matter.

This was a deathly difficult assignment. The Coal Worm paused for a moment, a thoughtful ghost, and then struggled to wrench the entire kit free from the wall. After a brief struggle and with a feeling of superhuman strength, the plastic tabs gave free from the oversized heads of the screws and he was holding his only chance.

He emptied the container into his satchel and continued upwards, this time with perfect technique and inexhaustible strength. He made the second and third rest ledges within the next four hours, and was nearly at the summit having only taken a single further dose as he huffed on the fourth ledge.

He could see the moonlit, starlit sky. It was obvious to anyone who had never seen the surface, the atmosphere. At night it was infused with light, even the darkest expanse.

So he climbed again, one more short burst, until he clambered up over the lip into an immediate crouch. Silent, completely immobile under the twilight, the Coal Worm was a statue. More soot than white remained of his suit, some sharper rocks had cut jagged wounds down his front. Some bled and others seemed to be shallow. He could still hear his blood spilling.

Satisfied after a pause, he took stock of his surroundings.

He saw the solar panels first. Large, tilted arrays that caught the sun which shot between broken buildings. At night, nothing moved. The buildings were, to him, foreign architecture. His handlers had allowed him to retain at least a little knowledge of life before. They were taller than one could imagine; they must have truly scraped the sky when they stood tall, proud, complete. Irregular rockpiles, snaking lines, led away from the arrays and then stopped, seemingly at random.

He knew that the rockpiles had been erected to protect the insulated cables beneath, those that carried power downward to the caverns below. The Coal Worm also had been told that these hasty constructs had been put in place by their ancestors who first made the decision to live subsurface, nearly two centuries ago – their knowledge had largely been lost... Strange othermen and mutants were said to skulk about; it was best never to linger in one place.

He saw none nearby. Keeping low to the ground, he

sprinted to the nearest array and took a look about. He had been to the surface many times before, but never at night – and never for more than a few minutes at a time, a half hour at most.

This assignment would last all night. If he lived that long. He could feel his heart thunder against his ribcage, threatening to burst free.

He felt the leather satchel slung at his hip, thrust his hand inside and rustled the contents. He felt the capped syringes, their plastic against his fingertips. Amongst the cold steel of his tools, his multitool wrench came to his grip and he pulled it free.

The chrome in his fist glinted in the moonlight like crystal.

He was mesmerized by the effect, shaking his head to clear his mind and take another furtive pan around to ensure he was still alone. The drugs were starting to lose their hold on his mind and the aches and ebbs of his flesh became more pressing.

Work first; then another dose. He had to ration them – only four syringes remained.

He made that promise to himself as he tightened his hold around the multitool and knelt next to the base of the solar array, using his free hand to softly wipe down a panel. He was looking for screws and he found them, then worked them free from each corner. Taking a deep breath and with whipcord straining muscles, he silently lifted the metal free and set it aside in the dust, leaning to.

The dispatch from the Elite had stated the intelligence on this array quite plainly – diagnostics were scant but indicated a few faults in the wiring leading from the power supply. Though it was the dead of night the great battery continued to pump some residual energy downward towards the city beneath; the wiring had seen better days and was still very much alive with electricity. So alive, in fact, that the Coal Worm could hear the hum of energy moving through space. He figured it best not to be a part of that space, and set to work with cautious expertise.

His hands moved like clockwork; he was intuitively adept at making the connections necessary to repair mechanical wounds. This was one of the reasons that he was the most senior Worm, the oldest and the grayest and the only one that had come back from the surface more than once.

He was finishing the repair and replacing the panel when he heard the voice behind him.

"I smell blood," came a gasping whisper at his back, almost breathing rotten down his neck.

He turned and fell back against the steel siding of the array, facing a ghoul. A sickening, half-eaten face contorted with hunger. Patchy hair and a grimy, naked body. Clutching a knife and coming for him, rasping, licking lips hungrily.

Fear energized him. He sprang from the path of the blade and gained his footing at some distance, readying his wrench. He rummaged into his satchel, felt the syringe, popped the cap, and pressed the needle to his thigh. The plunger fell while the wretch with the knife advanced slowly, a gravely bemused expression showing from dead eyes and a toothless maw.

No words. He felt an insane strength take hold; his confidence grew and he laughed like a madman as the ghoul swung a clumsy blow at his head. He dodged effortlessly, as a father playing with his son. Whipping the wrench —

weightless, he brought the chrome down across the ghoul's skull, splitting it in two.

There was a soft sound as the slight and depleted body of the abomination fell, then nothing. The moonlight shone upon the gore with no more comment than it made for other moments. The moon's cold illumination grew colder in grotesque. Even the Coal Worm turned quickly from it, wiping the tool on his suit and returning to replace the panel. It was not his first kill, and he was sure it would not be his last.

One job down. Two to go. One nearby on top of an "intact" skyscraper, or what remained of one. Structurally sound until the twelfth floor, open-topped from there and the perfect place for panels. It was also the perfect place for an ambush, or a squatter colony. The thoughts ran roughshod through his mind as he repacked his tool and kept his climbing hooks close at hand, jogging lightly out of the small circle of panels. He felt giddy, but retained enough sense to keep from laughing aloud as he ran through the darkness, through brick-spilled alleyways and torn-up streets.

He saw the building at the corner of a four way

intersection ahead, most streetlights long since bent and bowed, lying on the concrete. The telltale reflection of the moon and stars off the glass and steel of the array gave it away – and it seemed to attract the attention that he'd predicted. Campfires lit through the broken windows. Squatters were living in the building. Perhaps it was their home, since he was intruding upon their domain. It didn't matter to him; his objective was clear.

Stealing across the open street to hug the shadow afforded by haggard awnings and alcoves leading into various stores and offices, he crept along towards the weathered skyscraper. The wind blew down the corridor created by the broken buildings; the frost crept into his beard and what was exposed of his face with such strange sensation. His drugged mind struggled to focus on the task at hand, chomping at the bit to action and certain death.

He gripped the claws in his hands and, with firm and measured strikes, started scaling the side of the skyscraper. From his position in the long shadows, he knew he could get halfway there before emerging into the moonlight, becoming very visible to anyone who may glance in his direction. He hadn't seen any sentries or lookouts posted outside, however, nor had he encountered a living soul on his journey here. It was best not to invent problems before they emerged.

With an ear pressed against the wall, splayed against the siding a storey and a half from the ground, the Coal Worm could hear conversation muffled through concrete. Short, low barks of laughter punctuated by the higher timbre of women or perhaps children. He waited until the pauses between conversation were filled with bursts of chatter before making another move. His muscles began to shake and tremble despite his euphoria; his consciousness told him that blood loss and overall exertion were taking their toll despite the chemicals in his mind indicating otherwise.

He emerged from the shadows, crossed the threshold into the light. The image was impressionistic. He broke his cardinal rule and looked down. He saw streaks of his blood, black against the steel and cement. There were no voices here and he quickened his pace. Hand over hand, finding footholds, driving spikes and claws in, hauling his body upwards. The name Sisyphus floated into his mind and then flitted from it just as easily; he had read all of those old storybooks once. Both as a boy and to his own little girls, both long gone now. Gone from his life and, as he pushed the thoughts down inside, gone from his mind. The latter was a lie to himself. Lies kept his heart beating, and he believed them to be true with all of his spirit.

That was the way of the worm. It was his life now, until his life was a spent casing. His costume would be a husk and he would be elsewhere.

Crimson continued to flow from his wounds. The drugs thinned his blood. He would find no rest, but he would need to find bandages or else he'd not live out another hour.

He slipped. A hook came free, pulling a chunk of concrete with it. There was silence, a surreal, almost calm feeling as he swung free, twisting on one arm. The crack of the debris sounded as it crashed to earth, scattering. The echo was like a gunshot, pealing across the night and reverberating against piles of twisted rubble and the skeletons of old vehicles.

So much for silence. Scrambling to set his hook again, the Coal Worm immediately found purchase and moved with new purpose, spiderlike, cresting the jagged parapet of what stood as the top floor. At the same time, he could hear the patter of boots rushing from inside the building out onto the street below. Shouts, calls to one another, the alarm was raised as soon as they saw the debris and traced it back to the wall.

A wall streaked with blood leading to the rooftop.

Angry cries rang out in the night, the boiling tension of a human mob. Hunting an intruder into their territory — a threat to their women, their children, themselves.

The Coal Worm cursed violently, on his hands and knees, trying to regain his breath. Nobody shared the impromptu rooftop with him; an irregular edging of broken glass and empty steel framing that wilted like a dead flower as it reached pitifully towards endless, empty space. A futile symbol. He took it to heart and punched a fist into the gravel beneath his knees, screaming his rage against what was.

He hauled his body to his feet and staggered towards the second array; it was perched on a fabricated ledge, a large girder bolted and strapped to the frame. He clamped one claw around an eye and anchored himself as he stepped out onto the steel, crouching low as he hugged the array, working his way to the far side. He was beginning to feel very hot within his climbing suit. He knelt on the far side of the array and immediately saw the problem.

Initial intelligence reports guessed that the large diminishing of the power delivered by this panel — the power delivery had fallen from a high of 84% efficiency to something more like 12% over the last two months — was due to debris or dust covering the panel. No such thing.

The huge wires delivering the power from the solar array back down the tunnels had been spliced. The lights that the Coal Worm had seen through the gaping windows and holes of the squatters skyscraper were electric.

These people were not primitives, though their level of savagery was unknown. He didn't intend to stay long enough to find out.

Unluckily, as he began his work, kneeling low and beginning to sever the wires necessary to re-splice the power supply, the improvised shed door latched to the stairwell burst open. A stream of bodies came from below, taking up defensive positions behind piles of rubble and ancient piping. Taking only a few glances up as his hands worked furiously, he was struck by their apparent intelligence.

"Hey. Hey you. What the hell are you doing?" The English was thickly accented, strange and foreign to his ears. It took the Coal Worm a moment to even figure out what had been said to him. By that time, the voice had grown louder and more agitated.

"I said what the hell are you doing? If you don't stop, you're dead."

His hands stopped working. He peeked out from behind the array at the end of the girder, keeping as much of his body behind cover as possible.

"I don't want to hurt anybody," the Coal Worm said.

"You speak well enough for a caveman." The group laughed at the joke made by their leader. Now that the Coal Worm could see him, he was rather surprised to see a short man wearing patchwork clothing. They all wore the same handmade garments, stitched and mended from scavenged scraps. Some even held flashlights. His suspicions regarding their intelligence were confirmed.

"I could say the same of you."

"You turn that power off and you will hurt us. You'll kill us. Without the heat and the lights we will die. Even this..." The leader tossed his mane of salt and pepper hair — the light of the evening revealed him to be an older man — and waved a small handgun casually in front of him. "... won't stop too many of the beasts. Especially in the dark."

He had a gun. Rushing him was no option; this girder was too narrow and it was an awkward climb around the array. Besides, these people had offered him no harm. Yet.

"I can do this without cutting your power. I just need to take most of it. I can leave enough for what you need, and more."

The leader's wrinkled, sunspotted face came together in a pinched frown, skeptical.

"Don't believe a damn word he says. He's a sly and soft one, like all of the sewer rats," a female voice bawled out from the small mob scattered behind the short man.

"Yeah. I don't trust him. He's covered in blood already. Look at him!" shouted another voice, this time a reedy male from somewhere near the stairwell. He understood them through their thick accents.

The Coal Worm looked down at himself. The flashlights some of the men were holding had caught his chest. It appeared that he was still bleeding, though not as badly as before. The drug wore thin and some of his wounds closed.

"It's a long climb," was all he could muster in the face of their accusations. Hisses of derision and sputters of laughter could be heard for a moment before the sound of something else. Below, dragging noises. Moans.

As if forgetting the intruder was there, the leader turned his head and spoke to those behind him.

"Downstairs, quickly. Take positions. Get the women who fight armed and those who do not to shelter with the children."

The mob immediately scrambled to follow his orders; the reason became apparent to the Coal Worm as he cast a glance downward from his position at the end of the steel plank.

A shambling, irregular mass of dead and dying flesh was a wall moving toward their corner hideout. The loud noises, the scent of blood, friends of the ghoul he'd torn apart near the tunnel entrance – he was surely responsible for having

led them here. While the othermen may have suspected it —
most likely would have assumed it to be true even if it
wasn't — he couldn't help but feel a twinge in his gut, a
feeling that his shunt sought to strangle. It succeeded, for
the most part, and he breathed deep in relief, his chest
shuddering.

He fixed his attention on his work, his hands doing the
thinking for him as the rest of the world melted away.

He did not hear the first shots fired, did not see angry
snarling faces illuminated by muzzle flash. Again and again
in rounds, valuable bullets rained down from the pitch-black
windows of the depleted skyscraper. Several ghouls and
ghasts were punctured, black blood and bile streaming from
orifices, pitched to the concrete. For each that fell, several
nearby would stop to feed upon them. Shrieks and screams,
demonic insanity, an inversion of all that was *sacred*.

He felt his shunt whining inside of his skull, sweat
pouring from his brow. The unit seemed to be boiling his
mind, burning his brain from the inside out, blackening and
scorching the tissue. The processors pushed harder and
harder to save his sanity. He clenched his teeth, felt the

bone grind. His hands did not stop moving; they fulfilled his promise to the othermen as he tied their power off into a separate circuit. Wires were stripped and spliced and capped – old marettes and wire casings littered the oxidized steel, some fell loose to the rubble below.

The first of the undead had reached the threshold of the building, streaming up the narrow stairwell towards the chained steel doors at the front.

Without warning, a hail of debris and boiling water descended upon the crush at the front door. Two huge steel cookpots tumbled free from the window, spiraling steaming water which burned upturned eyes and faces. Old pieces of tech, displays, chairs, desks were hurled haphazardly, tying up the corpses and entangling those left struggling to break the door down.

"Blood! We will drink all of your blood! Your women! Your children! You will watch!" a hideous hag rasped. Her hair was in flames, curling and burning away, scorching what remained of her scalp. Her skull showed through. Both eyes were empty sockets. What force kept her bones animate was beyond the science that the Coal Worm knew.

The surface was a world outside of his understanding —
lethal and surreal and essentially unpredictable. He
wondered if he was hallucinating and then reminded himself
that he'd been long overdue for his dose, delayed by the
othermen and further delayed as they fought ghouls,
mutants, and demons for their lives.

Then came the glass bottles, the clear liquid, and the
flaming rag stuffed inside. Like freezing rain they broke
against the debris, the backs, the faces and the hands of the
demons. The flames were bright blue and then orange, not
white phosphorous but a torturous and slow end.

The netherwordly, sickening cries rose in intensity,
resounding and bending into further madness, echoing
against the husks of dead civilization. Clawed fingers raked
at torched clothing as it clung to skin, melting. The smell
was unbearable, and The Coal Worm retched even as he
caught a waft from below, a mixture of low-grade gasoline,
rotten burning meat, excrement, and viscera.

Half of the ghouls were dead, broken and charred bodies
strewn left and right down the poorly lit street and slumped
over the low bannisters of the stairwell. The rest had

withdrawn like scalded animals, pacing and tripping over each other, mumbling insanities. Those left standing were groaning loudly, promising vengeance and even more perverse tortures should they break that rusting chain and steel barrier separating them from the pure, those *alive*.

The Coal Worm pulled his multimeter free and attached the leads. The LED readout gave him some feeling of relief. He'd achieved an increase to 75% output; well above the requisite 50% of the mission parameter.

"Time to get the hell out of here," he uttered under his breath to no one in particular.

"They're still down there you know," came a little girl's voice, interrupting his descent. He peeked past the metal cube that was the base of the solar array and saw her.

She was maybe eight or nine years old, all freckles and strawberry-blonde wisps of hair, and she was perched, almost naturally, at the base of the girder.

"Don't worry about me. Get out of here. Find someplace safe."

"There's nowhere that's safe. Mommy and Daddy told

me that. Mommy still tells me that."

A bittersweet smile overtook him; he couldn't help but feel something for her.

"Mommy and Daddy were right, sweetheart."

"They say you are one of them. You live underground?" It was almost a question, a trembling child's search for truth from a stranger.

"Yeah. It's true. Lots of us live down there."

"And you aren't going to hurt us or steal from us?"

"No. No."

"How many of you are there... you know, down there? I had a friend who told me secrets once but she died. There are not many others my age to play with, and no girls. Boys play too hard and they can be mean."

"Mean? More than you can imagine. Girls can be mean, too. You'll know what I'm saying when you're older. And there are a million of us down there."

At this the little girl nodded sagely, even though she surely could not picture a million people in one place. In her sewn-too-many times jacket she shrugged off the heavy reality that faced her — everyday life.

"There are not a million of us here. I doubt I will live to be what they call *old*. When you wrinkle up and get grey hair. Most don't. Only Radiant and Shao in our clan. I am pretty old already. I'm nine. My name's Ree."

So he'd been a bit off in his guess, but not by much. As much as he wanted to stay and help these people, to learn more about the surface and the people he'd never knew lived there, he had a mission to complete. And if he didn't return, the investigative squads sent to follow his tracks would certainly find these squatters and eliminate them as a threat to the power supply.

"Ree. A nice name. Look Ree, I've got to go..."

"You can't. More are coming."

She lifted a small hand, the other clutching the edge of the rooftop, pointing at the flickering streetlights running away from the skyscraper.

It was another horde. Twice as large. Some were carrying pipes, sticks, and other crude weapons, advancing with purpose towards their position.

"You've got to get everyone out of here. There are too many to fight, and I have a feeling your leader has used all of his tricks."

Again, the wise nod, far beyond the years of her subterranean counterpart. At eight or nine most girls in the city beneath would be more concerned with trading the latest pop-holo or showing each other funny memes on the intranet. Not scavenging for clothing and fighting forces beyond mortal understanding.

"You're right. Mommy says we should have left weeks ago, but Radiant wants us to stay. So we stay. Whatever happens."

Radiant. The leader, he assumed.

This time it was his turn to nod to her, a silent goodbye. A frown stole over her face as if she expected a different outcome. A hero maybe.

Pulling another syringe from the satchel and quickly fitting it, he delivered his penultimate dose. Only one lonely needle remained in the bag. He felt the strength return to his limbs. He could no longer hear himself bleeding, and saw that his wounds held from weeping – for now.

He latched his hook to the fisheye underneath the girder. He shot Ree one last glance, a shock of black hair over emerald green eyes, and then he disappeared from her life.

She moved forward, biting her lip and holding her breath (although she didn't realize), edging along the girder, pressed against the flat metal casing of the generator.

When she got there, she saw a small pile of *something*. That was not her first concern. Splaying her legs and sitting astride the girder so she'd not fall, she leaned under, looking for a line or a hook leading to the mysterious stranger.

Nothing. Nothing but the pile that sat wrapped in front of her.

At first she thought it was simply a pile of rags. Then she reached for it and touched it. She realized it was wrapped in leather.

Pulling the bundle between her legs, her fingers deftly pulled at the leather, revealing its contents.

Three grenades; stock pins intact. She had been taught about all weapons since she was old enough to speak.

Two long knives – hunters tools – in a simple wooden

box, the box had some strange writing on it. It was not English. Or at least not English that Ree could read.

One syringe was filled with a clear liquid. Beside it, a scrap of paper and a pencil. This time she could read the letters.

"For your best men. Ones that aren't afraid to die. **No family?** [This was hastily scribbled out.] *Stronger. Into any vein. Enough for two or three. Give them a blade."* She read it quickly, making a few mistakes. Then below: *"You can't change the way it is, but you might change the way it will be."*

She gathered the bundle to herself, taking care not to prick her skin with the syringe even though it was loosely capped, and sprinted towards the stairwell.

Meanwhile, the Coal Worm was nearing the end of his descent, having climbed hand over hand on the underside of the girder, gripping the lips of the underside, then meeting the wall and making his way downward. He had made it to the shadowline long before the girl had made it to the end of the girder; he'd seen her tiptoeing along the side of the array towards where he'd disappeared.

He'd counted on her curiosity. He reached the ground and immediately began sprinting lightly, keeping close to the walls and awnings provided by the facades on his side of the street.

To his left was a stream of decomposing undeath. It was covered in filth. Creatures were gnawing at their own arms and picking the flesh from their faces. Cannibals, mutants, horrors.

Their distorted faces were obscured from view as cloud cover obscured the moon, the stars. Gunfire, burning barrels, and spare streetlights provided what little light remained. It felt natural to the Coal Worm – he could almost feel the anxiety emanating from the skyscraper.

He sparked the flare in his hand, flicking the cap free. The chemicals burned hot and the light was strong and intimidating, splashing against his battered frame. He looked almost as one of them.

Many broke ranks, enraptured by the gem of hissing light that bounced away from their prey. They tripped over decaying joints, tumbled into heaps. Some hefted their improvised weapons and with dull, grim expressions plodded on towards the makeshift stronghold held by the small group of squatters – othermen. Although they were not savages, dim and uncomprehending like the hosts they faced, but yet *other*. Another lie he'd been convinced of from on high, the Coal Worm thought bitterly to himself.

The Coal Worm led a stream of the cannibals away from their previous destination, keeping low to the ground and moving the flare at random to discourage any drunken potshots by those few holding zip guns or scavenged pistols.

The shots came nonetheless. Like staccato photographs from a media scrum, the barks of cheap weapons came from the line of beasts that peeled free of the procession. The Coal Worm felt the heat of a bullet pass by his face, striking the brick nearby, crushing it to powder.

He kept moving. There was no way he could face this many.

He pulled his hook into the palm of his right hand even as he held the flare in the left. The bullets continued to spark out from the shuffling mass, trailing him and swinging far wide as he made greater distance from the pack.

A few caught up to him, runners. Not as decayed as the rest, natural athletes in life, or supernatural strength – no time to think about it.

He heard their footfalls in an irregular pattern, catching up to him, growing closer.

He halted immediately, pivoting his hips and spinning the flare in front of their faces. They struggled to stop. The creatures of the night cowered in front of the chemical light. His hook caught one ghoul passing by, biting deep into their brain cavity. The Coal Worm yanked it free, bringing the bone with it.

Two more had sprinted past him, whirled on unsteady legs to face him, gnashed their teeth and pathetically tried to shield their eyes. Dropping the flare and rushing towards them, he gripped the hook with both hands. Crouched low and drove the point of the sharp metal hook into the belly of one undead, tearing it loose and all entrails with it.

He dropped the flare.

Then he continued off into the darkness, escaping the dying light of the flare as the abomination clutched at its own innards. The sole survivor turned to feed on his

221

downed brother.

Still, some followed him. Some stopped to prey upon their fallen brother, pushing the first out out of the way. The rest entered the darkness with him, a foot kicking the sputtering flare into a grate, into darkness.

This lent speed to his movements, the shudder in his chest was suppressed as his hormones and the drugs floating through his veins propelled him forward.

One objective left. Enough turns to lose the dull and dumb undead. Fifteen minutes at a run.

The minutes dragged on as the streetlights grew dimmer and fewer and farther between. He heard the sound of the grenades he had left behind exploding over the fading gunfire.

The nasty threats and demonic sounds spewed by his predators ebbed. The only sound now, with only a few minutes to go, was the hammering of his heart against his ribcage.

He knew they were still doggedly chasing him, frenetic and erratic, in the darkness.

There was no time to stop, to rest. The stimulants were masking symptoms starting to show through. He was covered in a sheen of sweat and blood and his climbing suit, once white, was burnt and shredded. His hooks were chipped and covered in black blood, ichor, and bile.

And he had only one dose left. His addict's mind was scrambling, illogical and unthinking.

Take it now. You're almost dead. You'll die if you don't take it now.

The urgings came and he fought them. His discipline, something he'd forged long before his capture, clamped down on his cravings, vice-like.

The last repair — and the most important — was at a hydroelectric dam that utilized the flow of a river that split the ancient city in twain as a source to generate power.

He emerged from a streetway to find himself on a waterfront, the perpendicular street he was standing on now meandering to match the curve of the great riverbanks. The water moved swiftly. He could see the current pulling branches and other floating debris.

The bridge that had once spanned the river hung, two limp wires, a broken ornament. It was like a drooping smile that crumbled, uneven and clashing. Waves lapped at the moorings. What failing light could struggle through the cloud cover etched these details, barely discernible in the Coal Worm's enhanced eyes. He saw the powerstation on this side of the river, just beyond the pieces of asphalt at the roadway's edge – and the steps downward to his target.

In a few scattered buildings on the far side of the river, he saw fires and lights in windows. There were more othermen, then. Many more, from the looks of it. He'd not been briefed on this as it wasn't necessarily pertinent to his assignment; he reasoned that the Elite must know already, however, given the growing frequency of surface resupply runs being conducted by the Huntress and her team.

He shook his head clear of these thoughts as he limped towards the rusted stairwell leading down into the substation. The heavy metal doors were shut, but not barred. Not a good sign from what he had seen so far this night.

As he reached the foot of the stairwell, he noticed the door was ajar. His fear worsened, the heat in his head reaching a fever and making him ill. He wobbled and caught himself against the steel door frame, nudging the door open with a slight creak.

He coughed, bringing the back of his hand to his mouth and pulling away yellow and black. His wounds had re-opened from the run. He suppressed a groan of agony, clenching his jaw.

Staggering into the blackness of the substation, the Coal Worm opened his satchel and found his light. The bright LED cast a pale white upon everything in the room instantly.

A row of computers, a few missing, with hastily pulled wires strung on the tabletop as the only evidence of what was. A thick layer of dust and pieces from the ceiling panels covered all surfaces. A small kitchenette in the far left corner, open concept, remnants of centuries-old food and brightly coloured cans. A coffee percolator. Heavy tomes tumbling free of a cheap tin bookshelf, sad and sagging.

He had a small pile of memory cards. These were a constant tertiary mission for any Coal Worm – data collection. He secured them in a special padded compartment in his satchel. Recovered data had led to numerous insights and breakthroughs for his people below. If he failed to survive the mission, anyone who found him would know where to look. If the ghouls didn't get to him first.

He forced his train of thought elsewhere. Such thoughts were for the defeated, the other worms he had stepped over, their bodies cold as he continued forward. He would make it.

He took another look around the small office. There was nothing of interest. Then he saw the hinge, opposite the kitchenette. Past that was a door, reinforced, leading to the right.

He moved through the room, nearly tripping on a chair, the soft faux-leather stripping away in his hand.

This door was also unlocked, even though it was trimmed with steel painted in caution stripes.

There were claw marks all over the door.

The harsh LED of his light caught them in sharp relief. He clipped the light to his shoulder and held both hooks at the ready, using the hook in his right hand to pry the trim of the door open.

It swung freely and noiselessly.

A damp, chill wall of air rushed to meet him. The sound of rushing water, white noise. The great gasps of his own breathing drowned out.

He panned the room with the light quickly. This revealed a natural cavern, and it was very different from his home. Jagged, toothlike rock formations adorned the ceiling. A metal grated walkway with ruined railing spanned rushing water. His forehead burned hot. He wiped at the sweat rolling from his brow, bringing stinging pain that woke his senses.

He crouched low and pointed his shoulder light at the large substation across the span, the heart of the huge turbines which roared at the far end of the cave. The clawmarks continued, scrawling their hatred all over the burnished and otherwise immaculate steel casing. It appeared the scavengers hadn't been able to gain access to the electrical innards, and so the Coal Worm heaved a sigh of relief, feeling at least some of the weight fall from his shoulders.

It was still possible.

The Coal Worm crept to the edge of the rickety looking bridge, dimming and focusing his light on the span. Though it too appeared to have been made from fine metal, either the minerals in the splashing water or falling rocks had punched ragged holes through the already narrow sheet at points.

Taking a tentative step, he felt the metal bend a bit toward the center. Nothing broke, only a slight creak. Another step, a long one, slowly setting down his weight, the exertion taking its toll. Now the surf rushed beneath him, subduing his inner thoughts. He took a long step. E moved just past the midpoint. The metal bridge groaned and the perforated grating beneath his boots began to flake free. He felt dizzy, again dissociated. The whiteness of the crashing water threatened to stupefy him.

A final step. The bridge snapped behind him, falling into the water.

He could feel the threat of weightlessness, the urging in the pit of his stomach as gravity pressed against nothing. He threw a leg out awkwardly, the spike at the tip of his boot scraping against the concrete uselessly.

He began to fall. He swung both hooks outward in an overhand motion, apelike. The hooks shrieked as they rent and clawed at the grating, tearing strips free.

Then catching, biting and holding. His arms snapped rigid and a bolt of pain shot through his upper body. He screamed despite himself, and continued to moan as he hung, twisting listlessly. The noise of the riverway buried his cries.

His boots touched the top of the whitecaps; he could feel a slight tug as the current pulled.

He tried to pull himself up. He could not. His muscles shook and trembled and failed.

The agony continued as his flesh was strained by his own suspended weight. The hooks in his palms, his hands covered in blood, bone showing through in places. A weakening, white knuckled grip with bruises blooming like vines along his wrists.

He used the last of his strength to deliver hard kicks to

the smooth siding of the wall, just above the waterline. He pushed himself up a few feet closer to the lip of the wall. The spikes drove deep and, with three points of contact, he could breathe for a few moments.

He hung his head in despair and considered what options were left to him.

It was now or never. The final dose found its way into his left hand as a look of intensity came over him and he tapped his vein. He felt the liquid strength enter him once more. The knowledge that it would be his last chance was overwhelmed by a newfound confidence.

With precise strikes he used the spikes on his boots to bear most of the weight as he pushed upwards, adjacent to the hanging skeleton of the bridge. He could not place any real amount of weight on the collapsed bridge for fear of an uncontrolled fall, using his hooks on the grating only to steady himself as his legs did the work.

He made it, gaining the ledge and pushing himself into a crouch. He noticed now that his light had been smashed when he'd struck the concrete wall of the turbine moorings in his fall.

Only two diodes of the inline six remained, showing bare through the open facing of the light on his shoulder.

It would have to do. The small spot of light showed the erratic etching on the opposing panel, but it would take some time to loosen all of the bolts.

Pulling his multitool free, he set to work. The bolts were a bit rusted, and some had been stripped away by scavengers or ghouls. Nonetheless, the kit came prepared, whether grease spray or boltbore was necessary. The drug pushed his mind into a state of perfect consciousness, each movement fluid and prepared.

The panel was off in less than five minutes, lain to the side.

A simple repair, despite how difficult the trek to get here had been. A few disconnects from an old battery. The replacement battery, sealed in clamshell plastic, installed and reconnected. The wiring diagrams appeared in his mind's eye and he executed them.

The battery was holding charge. The panel was replaced, and the bolts that could be salvaged were reset, with lock-tight applied.

Now to make it back alive. He was on an island. On three sides of this mooring, water. The side to his left met the cavern wall. The natural shape of the ceiling meant that he would have to trek at least part of the way overhand, in suspension. Despite the drug, his muscles ached in anticipation.

The darkness enveloped him, the twin diodes on his lamp giving little respite against advancing shadows.

The sharp, layered rocks were his only path home. His heart raced as he realized they were largely slate and shale; he cursed the foolish engineers and architects of the surface for their lack of foresight. Great veins of stronger igneous stones, like granite or conglomerate, showed through in clusters.

Action was in the heart of the Coal Worm and he strode to the cavern wall and began his ascent. He had little time to test each foothold and handhold, merely tugging at the straps and bouncing lightly as he worked his way upward.

Pain was an illusion to him.

He felt something cool run from his nose and over his lips. His tongue darted out and tasted iron. He took a deep breath and expelled it through his nostrils, clearing them, the blood dotting his neck and collarbone. He continued, reaching the ceiling.

He cast his gaze about amongst the stones for something solid.

He found something shining, a bit of quartz. He struck it, felt the hook hold true, and swung.

As he did, the small arc of his light revealed white forms, long nails and claws pinching into the rock.

"Blood," they hissed at him, and then came at him.

A blur and his head was struck to the side and he bobbed on his suspended arm harshly. He raised his free hand and felt another sharp blow rake across his forearm, tearing flesh free.

Then, a sickly warmth as the small white ghoul lept from the ceiling and caught his free arm, adding more weight which tore at the muscles and bone supporting them both. Eager eyes flashed in the dim light, bright fangs that were revealed for a moment before driving into the gore of his forearm.

He screamed, violently shaking his arm, achieving nothing. His screams echoed within the cavern, competing with the waves and what sounded like rasping laughter coming closer. Something broke inside – and rage consumed him.

He swung his ravaged arm, the ghoul hanging on, towards his right leg – twisting and kicking as he did so. The spike caught the creature, still feeding with fangs attached, in the ribcage. It punched through, a sickening snap; the ghoul yanked its head up in mute surprise.

Then it fell free, splashing noiselessly. He spun on his remaining hook and saw another ghoul less than ten feet away. He would not fight here. The leather straps and chains attaching his hooks to his wrists were intact despite his ruined forearm. He had no time to look for granite.

He swung forward at a madman's pace, driving his hooks into hanging rocks. The Coal Worm could hear the deathly chuckling of the albino beast in pursuit. Some stones crumbled the second that he was free of them, some held.

When he had nearly reached the wall, he traversed through the air spread-eagled, the impact temporarily driving the air from his lungs. He absently and awkwardly drove the spikes into the wall twenty feet from the floor.

The seconds it took him to recover were nearly fatal as he felt a heavy weight strike the back of his suit and sharp pains as claws rent through it, into his back.

The Coal Worm allowed himself to fall free, backwards, cradling his head with his hands. The ghoul continued to tear at his back mindlessly. Then they struck the floor, flat. His weight crushed the monster. He could feel its skull cave and burst beneath his back.

He coughed, hard, his lungs struggling to find air. Brackish liquid spilled from between cracked lips; he wheezed and hiccuped.

Run. He had to run if he wanted to live. His body would give anything to be free of the pain. His shunt was cold and dead inside of him, misery unaccompanied.

So the Coal Worm rolled over, onto his hands and knees. Spit up some more filth. Shuddering and looking like a dead man, gaining his feet.

Get up the stairs. Go through the caution-trimmed door.

Pausing a few moments, he rested in the kitchenette for precious seconds to gain a few breaths. Bursting from the door and upwards, he went away from the riverbank and again down the alleyway, the same way he'd came.

His gait was awkward and uneven, his breathing ragged. The last dose burned fumes within him, his own rage enkindling the chemical cocktail.

Almost there. Only a few hundred meters to go.

On a small side street, he was stopped in his tracks.

A lanky ghoul, naked, crouched low, hunkered over a meal, pawing meat into its mouth from a stomach cavity.

There was a uniform on the corpse. Huntress' enforcers. A gun was clenched tight in the dead woman's fist.

Gunfire sounded, the deep bark of a higher calibre weapon punctuating smaller weapons.

He swept shadowlike towards the ghoul, ignorant of its impending doom. The hook caught it in the rotting strands of skin covering its throat; he tore it free and the backbone with it.

The Coal Worm let the gorey hook hang free and pried

the gun from dead fingers. The drugs were fading fast and he was on the verge of collapse. Remaining upright was a struggle.

Just a bit further. He focused on the brickwork passing by, trying to keep his mind from anything but his suffering. To stop was to die, eaten alive by ravenous and perverted cannibals. It was not an option as long as he breathed.

His lungs rattled. He'd stopped sweating some time ago.

The gunfire grew louder as he came closer to the tunnel downwards. He saw the lightning of muzzle flashes painting nearby buildings at the end of the street. He limped his way there, keeping the pistol at the ready.

He emerged at the end of the street. A bent STOP sign and Eucalyptus Avenue pointing skyward on a forest green sign, mottled now. In the background, he saw them. They came into focus.

The Huntress, her mahogany-stock automatic shouldered, booming death. Her beautiful, pale-skinned face made even more erotic by the twist of painted lips as she pulled the trigger. Wisps of pure blonde hair were matted with blood to her face.

The Elite guardsmen were her enforcement detail. Dozens of them, pistols popping off rounds at a tangled ring of mutants. Some had fallen, many more fought. Like before, the beasts were singlemindedly feeding upon their kill despite the danger.

There were hundreds of dead demons, their misshapen faces and scabrous skin shining wet and black. Moments of gross expression flashed at him, totemlike, as he neared the edge of the circle, the backs of the beasts to the Coal Worm.

Distracted, delirious, the Coal Worm sought a break in the shifting circle to break through to his superiors. A chance to live to see another day.

This time he did not hear them coming, nor smell them. He felt them coming, something intangible.

He turned with a grim smile on his lips, haggard, barely standing. His eyes were dull and stonelike.

The pistol bucked in his hand. Flames spewed from the barrel and hot metal erupted.

The first bullet was a clean shot, above the bridge of the nose. A hissing abomination died at his feet a few feet away.

More were coming. He pulled the trigger again and again. The second and third rounds stitched across the chest of another ghoul, the wounds exploding, knocking the thing down. The third and fourth punched through rotten flesh, downing another ghoul.

The click of an empty chamber, a useless trigger.

His hooks clenched in his hands – they fell upon him, crashing down on the Coal Worm like a wave. He fought to keep his footing as he slashed out at feral faces. He tore and ripped at them as they did the same to him.

A blow took him in the kneecap. A sharp, blinding pain. He gasped and cried out as he fell to the earth, feeling filthy fingernails pry at his skin, his beard, clawing it free of his face.

The cannon's roar of a large calibre rifle. Something hot and wet splashing down onto his upturned face, stinging his own wounds.

A body fell on him, pinning him. His ear pressed to the earth, the Coal Worm heard the muffled report of the Huntress' rifle beat out a deadly parade. More dull thuds.

A woman's voice screamed orders, high and confident and urgent.

A weight lifted from him. His lungs tasted air, he coughed and vomited on himself. Strong hands yanked at his arms, dragging him, his boots leaving a rut in the soft earth.

Gunfire, fire and heat. Grenades, explosives, and curses. The sound of boots beating the ground about him.

"Back! Back! We need him!" the Huntress shouted.

He struggled to open his eyes but could not. His mouth was filled with rot. His body was broken and the drugs had left him depleted. He tried to see again, eyelids flickering, muscles straining. He opened his eyes. Blurred shapes and forms. The colours of the Elite, uniformed men. Black gloves. The bright white armour of the Huntress, alone against a few remaining enemies — even as he watched she put them down with a roar.

She turned to him, covered in her own blood and the gore of her kills. A strange smile stole across her ruby lips. Chemical flame burned atop already charred grass. He was struck by her beauty. He returned the secret smile.

Then they pulled him down, across the ledge, into the tunnel.

The Coal Worm gave himself over to his wounds. His jaw fell to his ravaged chest. His tortured muscles went limp. His heart beat weakly.

Green eyes dimmed, shut, then melted into the black.

THE AUTHOR'S RESPECTS

To all those who've fallen a few times and are still trying to make it to the surface.

A few shout outs here to inspirations. A few tokens of respect. But only a few. My family. Mom, Dad, Luke. My heart and my soon to be wife, Jessica. My other brothers and sisters in the same way. We walked together for a while. Everyone out there hustlin'. I know that shit is hard. People out there standing up for themselves. Dolph Lundgren. Too many early science fiction writers to list in one acknowledgement. Heavy metal. The promise of warm sunshine and the ocean breeze. Nova Scotia and Newfoundland. Lettin' 'er rip.

Special thanks to Ms. Amanda-Leigh MacLeod for her editorial services, and to Ms. Christina Majaski for the moral support. Oh yeah -- and Shawn Butler for watching a week straight of superhero cartoons during his first trip to Nova Scotia which inspired "Sick Divine." That's the seed that would eventually bear the story for the book you're holding in your hands right now.

Keep an eye out. I'm not done wordslinging yet.

Nicholas Morine

THE AUTHOR IN BRIEF

Nicholas Morine is hard as fuck. This is his bio.

The author was born and raised in Gaspereau, Nova Scotia. As a wee child, Nicholas would often steal apples from a nearby orchard, egged on by his gramps.

The boy from Gaspereau later ventured to St. John's, Newfoundland, seeking an education. There, he found a new wolfpack to run with and his foxy mate. He also attained the most potent of degrees, as he is now a Master of Philosophy in Humanities.

Metal is his religion. He is a member of Ebon.

Words are his livelihood. He has written many words on a range of subjects, from tech to fashion. Having returned to Nova Scotia, he continues to write non-fiction and fiction. Montag Press published his debut novel, *Punish the Wicked: A Dystopian Horror*. Problematic Press is proud to present *Cavern: City in the Dark*, his second novel. The author promises more words will come.

Problematic Press is a small, independent book publishing endeavour based in St. John's, NL. Problematic Press has a mission with a broad scope, aiming to entertain and educate readers of all ages.

Perhaps that's problematic. Problems make us think.

http://problematicpress.wordpress.com

James De Mille's *A Strange Manuscript Found in a Copper Cylinder* is one of the first Canadian texts to explore science fiction. 125 years after its release, this tale is still sure to thrill and excite audiences!

Vester Vade Mecum: A Collection of Short Fiction includes works by such authors as Washington Irving, Edgar Allan Poe, Mary Shelley, Oscar Wilde, Arthur Conan Doyle, Pauline Hopkins, plus others! This anthology revisits many classic tales that remain surprisingly relevant today. Enjoy!